CADE

SEALs of Steel, Book 3

Dale Mayer

Books in This Series:

CADE: SEALS OF STEEL, BOOK 3
Dale Mayer
Valley Publishing Ltd.

Copyright © 2018

ISBN-13: 978-1-773360-78-2
Print Edition

About This Book

When an eight-man unit hit a landmine, all were injured but one died. The remaining seven aim to see his death avenged.

A hit-and-run investigation leads Cade to a connection to the landmine explosion.

While at the bedside of her best friend in a coma, Faith meets Cade, who asks about the accident. She learns her relationship with her friend has put her in a killer's sights. Suddenly, Cade's nightmare becomes her own...

Your Free Book Awaits!

KILL OR BE KILLED

Part of an elite SEAL team, Mason takes on the dangerous jobs no one else wants to do – or can do. When he's on a mission, he's focused and dedicated. When he's not, he plays as hard as he fights.

Until he meets a woman he can't have but can't forget. Software developer, Tesla lost her brother in combat and has no intention of getting close to someone else in the military. Determined to save other US soldiers from a similar fate, she's created a program that could save lives. But other countries know about the program, and they won't stop until they get it – and get her.

Time is running out ... For her ... For him ... For them ...

DOWNLOAD a *__complimentary__* copy of MASON? Just tell me where to send it!

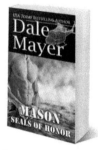

http://dalemayer.com/sealsmason/

PROLOGUE

CADE TERENCE LIFTED his bag and threw it over his shoulder as they walked out of the airport. He glanced at Talon. "You didn't have to come back with me."

Talon shrugged. "I want to see Badger anyway. Laszlo is coming in on the next flight, so I think we should have a meeting. If Badger is up to it."

"We might have to meet in his hospital room. But you know how he'll feel if he's kept out of the loop."

Talon nodded. "I think it's time the others knew too."

"Erick's ahead of you. He already brought Geir in on this. I don't know what the hell's going on, but I swear to God it isn't any of us."

"I'm of the same opinion," Talon said. "But we must find out who it is."

Just then some of the airline crew walked out to a cab pulling up for them.

Cade looked over at Talon. "You have wheels?"

Talon shook his head. "No. Do you?"

Cade shook his head. "We can grab a cab if you want."

The cab pulled away with the airline crew members just as another uniformed woman walked out. "Oh, drat."

Cade looked at her. "Did you miss your taxi?" She was dressed in the same airline attire as the crew members who had just left.

"Yeah. It figures. It seems like I'm always late these days." She smiled up at them. "That's all right. I'll get the next one."

Another taxi pulled up just then. Cade motioned to her. "Go ahead."

She laughed and flashed him a smile. "I'm not sure where you guys are going, but I'm heading downtown, if you want to share a ride."

"Sure, sounds good." They waited for her to get in the front of the taxi, and then they got in the back. As she gave instructions to the driver, Cade realized they lived within a few blocks of each other.

"We're heading close to the same area anyway," Cade said.

She turned to look at them. "Have you two been traveling long?"

They smiled. Cade said, "Just a few days. But I'm happy to be going home."

She nodded. "I feel the same way. I have been with the company for a long time now. With all the traveling I do, sometimes it's just nice to come home and to stay home."

"Home is Santa Fe?"

"It is. What about you guys?"

"I'm Santa Fe. Talon's been all over the world. Not sure he has a home anymore," Cade said in a teasing voice.

Talon laughed. "Bought a house. Fixing it up is my day job."

"At least you have that. I live alone. I don't have any family here at all," she said. She reached out a hand over the front seat. "I'm Faith, by the way."

The men introduced themselves. Cade looked at her for a long moment. "You look familiar."

She raised an eyebrow. "Well, you did just get off a flight. It was probably one I was on."

He shook his head. "No, I would have seen you moving up and down the aisles."

She laughed, a sound of pure joy and amusement. "No, you wouldn't have."

He glared at her suspiciously. "Why not?"

"Because," she said gently, "I'm the pilot."

CHAPTER 1

O NCE LASZLO HAD flown into town, and Erick had joined them all at Cade's place, their plans to go straight to Badger's side flew out the window as soon as Cade got the text from Kat.

No meeting. Badger is in intensive care. He won't be coming out anytime soon.

Cade stared at the phone.

Erick sat beside him in the two matching armchairs. Laszlo and Talon were on the couch opposite them. "What's up?"

Cade shared the message as he dialed Kat's number. When Kat answered the phone, he asked, "What happened?"

"Blood clot," she said, her tone dark, low. "It was touch-and-go there for a while. It still is, in fact. I'm at the hospital now. But whatever plans you were hoping to include him in, he'll pass for now. When he pulls out of this, he has to have surgery again."

"He'll pull through," Cade said. "He's pulled through everything so far."

She said, "Absolutely he has. And I certainly won't let him give up. But he should have had the surgery a long time ago."

Cade could hear the sadness in her tone.

With speakerphone on, Erick, Talon and Laszlo could

also hear the conversation, and, from the mixed looks on their faces, Cade knew exactly how they felt. "Can we come see him?"

"Nobody can see him. Only family. And he doesn't have any of that anymore."

"We're his family," Cade said in a harsh tone. "So are you, Kat."

"They're allowing me in. But only because he seems to be calmer when I'm there. I don't know if you have any pull at the hospital and can get yourselves in to see him. If not, what you should do is carry on with what matters to Badger most. And that is finding out who did this to all of you. But he can't run point. And I know you need someone to keep communications open and coordinated."

Cade stared off into space. Kat was right, but solving this issue would take a group agreement from the rest of the team.

"Levi and Mason need someone as their main contact. There have even been calls from a Merk and a Brandon. I don't know who half these men are," she said. "Plus I can't just leave my business. I'm working at the hospital as often as I can so I can check up on Badger. Otherwise I'm at the office. Badger isn't conscious—he won't likely wake up for a little while. The doctors are hoping tomorrow. But they've given him drugs. Every time he surfaces, he fights to get out of the bed. He's caught up in his own nightmares. They're keeping him sedated until his body gets through the worst of it."

"Don't you worry. We'll fix this," Cade promised. "We'll get back to you as to who'll handle what. Your job will be to keep us in the loop on Badger's condition."

"My job is to keep him alive," she said softly. "But I can

also keep you in the loop." With that she hung up.

The men just stared at each other, a somber pall falling over them. At the moment, four of the remaining seven of their former unit were gathered here. Talon, Cade, Erick, and Laszlo—who'd only arrived a couple hours ago.

Honey walked over and sat beside Erick on the arm of his chair and slid her fingers through his good hand. "I know you must go back out," she said, "but I need to be here for Kat."

A little late but Erick realized how hard this was on her too. He squeezed Honey's fingers and glanced around at the other men. "Suggestions?"

Talon said, "We do what we set out to do. We'll find the asshole who did this to us."

"Yes, but we need a new man to stay here to run point. Like Kat said, there're a lot of phone calls. Somebody has to be our communications center." Cade watched as Honey glanced over at Laszlo and Talon and saw the same answer in their gazes. Cade turned to Erick and said, "And you're it."

Anger flashed in Erick's face.

Cade shook his head. "No, no arguments. You have to step up and take Badger's place."

"I have no problem stepping up," Erick growled. "But you're not putting me in a babysitting position."

Cade saw the relief in Honey's face. "And you have something else to consider," he said gently. He picked up his coffee cup and looked at it. "Why is the coffee always gone?"

Honey bounced to her feet. "I'll put on some more. Sounds like we'll need another couple pots." And she disappeared.

Immediately Cade leaned forward and said, "Erick, you must also consider Honey."

Erick glared at them, but Cade saw the awareness in Erick's eyes. "None of us have a partner but Badger and you. We've made a lot of mistakes in our lives, and we've paid some pretty major prices already. But you also have a chance of something very special here. Kat is here for Badger. Honey needs to be here for Kat, and you need to be here for Honey. You are the obvious point man."

Erick wanted to argue. The anger and frustration was evident on his face. But then his own phone buzzed. He glanced at it. "It's Levi. He wants an update. Actually," Erick said, "his words are, *What the hell is going on?*"

Cade settled back. "Exactly."

"Still there's nothing for me to run point on if we don't have the next step determined," Erick said, holding his phone but not yet answering.

"Has anybody heard from Geir?" Talon asked, then turned to Erick. "You already contacted him, didn't you?"

"I did. And then he went silent."

The men straightened.

Talon demanded, "How long ago?"

Erick checked his phone. "Twelve hours."

Instantly the air became charged. "That's too long."

"I know."

"And that's another reason why you need to run comms," Laszlo said quietly. "In our heads we were still thinking about Badger, that he would keep track of this. What if Geir is in trouble?"

"Geir has always been very good at getting out of trouble," Talon reminded the group. "But twelve hours of silence is too long, even for him."

Erick pulled out his phone and called Geir. "Still no answer."

"But the phone is ringing?" Laszlo grabbed his laptop and opened it up. "Give me the number."

As Erick read it off, everybody entered Geir's number into their cell phones.

As he did so, Cade wondered aloud, "Why is it I don't have this number?"

"Geir has been out of touch for the last few months. In many ways it was hard to reach him because he just bounced around." Erick stretched out his legs.

"This phone number he contacted you on is no longer valid," Laszlo said.

"A burner phone?"

"That would be my guess." Laszlo nodded. "The only reason for him to do that is if he didn't want to be tracked," Laszlo said.

"Is there any chance he's been thinking the exact same thing as Badger?" Talon asked. That was the big question in front of them. "Did he say anything to you, Erick?"

"Not really. I just told Geir that we were setting up a face-to-face meeting, and it was important. It had to do with two years ago."

"His response?"

"*On it.*"

The men stared at each other.

Talon whispered, "Shit."

"When he said that, I thought his wording meant, he was on his way here."

"Instead he's already on it. As in, he's tracking down what the hell's going on too."

Inside Cade wanted to jump for joy. Geir was one of the good guys. Hell, all seven of them were good guys. "And there's no way he's guilty of blowing us up if he's out hunting."

"None of us are responsible for our land mine accident," Talon said quietly. "I suggest we all come to that agreement right now. All seven of us are innocent. There's another explanation. We just don't know about it yet."

The men nodded and, as one, said, "Agreed."

"Always had that position," Laszlo said quietly. "Four of us are here. Badger is in the hospital. That's five. Geir is six. What about Jager?" He glanced from one face to the other. "Anybody heard from him?"

"I know his parents died recently," Talon said. "I haven't heard anything further."

Erick's voice, when he spoke up, was cautious, though still a lot of anger and frustration was in it. But he had come to terms with the worst of it. "I'm just throwing this out there because I think it needs to be brought up, and I'm not sure if you guys have thought of it."

The men glanced at him.

Erick locked his gaze on Cade's. "There's been a lot of death in our families in the last two years."

Cade straightened. "What are you saying?"

"My older brother was found dead in his vehicle at his office. He had a weak heart already, and, after a supremely bad day at work, he had a heart attack in his vehicle. He was fourteen years older than me. And not in great health, so it was terrible, as he was still so young, but almost understandable. And that was well over a year ago now, likely fourteen months or so." Erick slumped as Honey returned with the coffeepot on a tray. He smiled up at her. "Thanks, sweetie."

She nodded, quickly poured out the coffee for all of them. "I'll be working in the kitchen. I'll leave you guys to it." And with a bright smile she turned and left.

He waited until she was out of earshot before he turned to the others. "Badger's parents were killed six months after our land mine explosion. Jager's parents were killed." He turned to look at Laszlo. "Any idea when?"

"About four months ago."

"So, eighteen months ago and then four months ago we have two sets of parents gone. Anybody else lose somebody in this time frame?"

Cade let out a slow and steady breath. It was too hard to contemplate.

But Erick looked at him with a knowing eye. "Your sister. She died in what? A multicar pileup a couple of winters ago, right?"

Slowly, ever-so-slowly, as if a bigger movement would make him splinter into pieces, Cade nodded. "But that was seventeen months now."

"That breaks the pattern. It wasn't your parents," Laszlo said. And then he froze. "And that's because you don't have any, do you? They were already dead, right?"

Cade nodded. "My sister was my last remaining family member," he said softly. "We lost our parents when I was in high school. It's one of the reasons I went into the navy. I was looking for a family."

Erick squeezed his shoulder. "And you found it. Keep that thought in place."

Cade couldn't think of anything but his sister. He stared at Erick. "Is this just a wild guess?"

"Too much death for it all to be a coincidence." Erick glanced at Talon. "Have you lost anyone in the last couple years since the explosion?"

Talon frowned. "I don't have anything to do with my family. I was a foster kid way back when. I know my birth parents are out there but don't know who they are, don't know any of the details."

"And your foster care family?" Erick asked.

"You mean the last one?" He shook his head. "I haven't seen or heard from them in years."

"Check to see if they're still alive," Erick said quietly. "Maybe, if they weren't close to you, they weren't targeted."

Cade studied Laszlo's face. "Laszlo, you're not talking."

Laszlo lifted his face, a funny look in his eyes. "I didn't lose anyone," he said quietly. "My mom's been gone for years. But my father was recently in a car accident, and we nearly lost him."

"How long ago?"

"Just a month back."

Silence filled the room.

Cade felt something inside splintering a little further with every word. "So it's not enough that we were targeted? But now you're saying our families have been targeted too?" He stared at the others. "That's hate at a whole new level."

"It is. It is indeed."

They each picked up a coffee cup, lost in their thoughts and memories.

"Laszlo, you were with your father before you came here?"

Hi face grim, Laszlo said, "My brother is with him. At first it was my father looking after my brother. Now it's more about my brother looking after my father."

"You may want to add some protection detail—at least give your brother a warning."

"My brother isn't capable of looking after both of them. He's been dealing with cancer treatments this last year. He's in remission now, but he's weak. In fact, he and my father are both vulnerable." He put down his coffee cup with a bang, stood to pace. "I need to go home," he said quietly.

"I think I should come with you," Cade said. "Do you have the details on your father's accident?"

Laszlo turned to look at him. "Only what the police told us. Now I want the full report."

"Do you know who hit him? Do you know any other details?"

"My father always went for a walk in the evening. Always. For almost all of his seventy-four years he had dinner, then would go for a walk."

"Don't tell me the accident happened while he was walking?"

"Hit-and-run," he growled. "Nobody knows anything about the vehicle. Nobody saw the vehicle. Nobody saw the accident. The dogs came home, barking, brought my brother outside to see what had happened. My brother found our father and got him to the hospital."

"What kind of shape is he in?" Erick asked quietly.

Shoving his fists into his pockets, Laszlo rocked back on his heels. "It's bad," he admitted. "Head injury, several broken ribs, broken leg and hip. He's out of the hospital now, at home, but he's mostly immobile. I didn't want to leave them. But, once I realized what was going on here, no way I wouldn't come and help too. My father's recovering. Nurses come to the house every few days to check on him. Plus he has my brother. Only now a killer could be coming after our father to finish the job he started."

Laszlo's jaw clenched, a muscle in the side of his face twitching. "And maybe we're off in the deep end here," he said. "Absolutely nothing says that the person who blew us up two years ago is going after our families. What about that makes sense?"

"Like Cade said," Talon offered, "it's hate. At a whole new level."

"But it's not just hating one of us. It means hating all of us."

"We need to find out from Geir if he sustained any family losses," Erick said abruptly. "While we already know about Jager's parents' deaths, contacting Jager for any further info will be a whole different problem—if we can't get a hold of him yet."

"If he's gone dark, you know you can't reach him unless he wants to be reached."

"We might not get a response, but we can certainly get a message to him. The same as I did for Geir," Erick corrected. "And I can do that. I can text him to find out if he's had any personal losses and to say we're worried about a new angle."

"Do that now. I'll book a flight," Laszlo said. "No way I'm leaving my father and brother alone. Not right now. Not like this. Of all the things they are capable of doing, defending themselves against a pro is not one of them."

"It's also potentially our closest lead to finding out who did this to all of us," Cade said. "Make sure you book a flight for me too."

Talon snorted. "No way in hell you two are leaving me behind. If they've already tried to take out your father, then we all have some work to do."

"This just got exponentially bigger," Erick protested. "We need every one of those accident reports." He almost growled, then sighed. "Since I'm now the official comm center"—he glared at the other guys—"I'll need details from each of you as to when and where and who. I'll arrange to get copies of the official reports from the respective police departments and the coroners, as needed. We'll compare all the details, and we'll need everybody's help to deal with what we find."

"We already know Levi and Mason will help," Cade said. "And they have some of the best computer equipment and the best programmers to go with it. Let's pull all the information, toss it into one of their laps and see if they can come up with any correlations. At the same time, the three of us will fly to Norway and make sure that accident was exactly that. An accident."

FAITH STARED AT the email in her inbox. It was from Mary, the sister of her best friend, Elizabeth. She and Faith had gone to school together in Santa Fe, New Mexico. But when Faith went into flight school, Elizabeth's mother had remarried and moved to Norway. It was where Elizabeth had been born, so she had decided to return to her home country and to become a teacher there, so she could stay close to her mom and sister.

Faith read it aloud slowly. "*So sorry to tell you but Elizabeth was in a bad car accident. She's alive and holding on, but the prognosis isn't good.*"

Faith reached for her phone, grateful Mary had at least included her phone number. When Mary answered, Faith said, "I'm flying over."

"I can understand maybe you want to do that," Mary said. "But she's not awake and isn't likely to regain consciousness. She's dying."

Faith pinched the bridge of her nose. It was all she could do to not burst into tears. "When did this happen?"

"Yesterday," Mary said sadly. "Accidents are like that. They take the best of us and wipe them off the face of the earth with absolutely no apologies."

Faith hated that it was already a done deal in Mary's mind. "I can be there in twelve hours." She checked her watch. "Maybe less."

"I know you're a pilot, but you need a plane to make it that fast."

"I can probably get on the next flight. I'll send you the details as soon as I know them." Faith hung up with Mary as she raced to her bedroom, already calling the flight office. "I need a compassionate leave flight to Norway yesterday," she snapped.

"Family?"

"Best friend."

Being a pilot for the company, she already got free flights. But often overseas flights were fully booked. She just prayed for a miracle.

"We have one leaving in forty-seven minutes. But that's likely too early for you."

"No, it's not. I'll take it."

She hung up the phone, threw a few pieces of clothing into her carry-on bag, grabbed her passport and purse, thankful she was always ready to go at a moment's notice, and raced for her vehicle. She briefly thought about calling for a cab, her mind remembering the two men she'd met in her last cab ride.

She vaguely remembered their names. She remembered the blond, blue-eyed man more. But then he had one of those faces that left an impression. Eyes that seemed to gaze into her soul, looking for something, always searching for answers. Inside her car she opened the garage door with the remote, drove out, hit the button to close the door behind her then pulled out onto the main road. As soon as she reached the open highway, she stomped on the gas pedal.

She didn't have time for any delays. They wouldn't hold the plane for her either. It's not like she's flying this one. She was only fifteen minutes away from the airport on purpose. This was her life. She was out far enough to be in a suburban area but still close enough that she didn't have a horrible drive getting in and out of work. She left her vehicle in long-term parking any time she could. That was where she headed now.

She parked and ran through the departure lanes. She cleared security easily and raced toward the departure gate. The gate attendant looked up, saw her and cried, "Oh, thank heavens. Everyone's boarded."

She nodded and barreled through. As soon as the onboard flight attendant saw her, she motioned her in, pointed at the front seat and said, "That's yours," and proceeded to close the door behind her.

Faith tossed her bag in the overhead compartment and collapsed into the seat, her breath ragged, her hands trembling.

An older lady was seated beside her. "So you're the one we were waiting for."

Faith slanted her gaze at the woman and whispered, "Sorry."

The older lady just smiled and nodded. "When you get to be my age, very few things in life are worth racing for."

"A friend is dying."

"Oh, my dear." The woman grabbed her hand to hold it in both of hers. "I'm so sorry."

The tears she hadn't allowed herself to shed clung to the

corner of her eyelashes. She sniffled, reached into her purse and pulled out a Kleenex. "I just got word," she said. "It's all I could do to grab this flight, so I can get over there."

She gently withdrew her hand and settled into her spot. She had brought her laptop with her, and, as soon as the flight was at altitude and stable, she sent messages to move her work shifts around. She'd taken shifts from many coworkers, and thankfully they were happy to return the favor. Then Faith sent an email to Mary, saying when she would arrive. The next nine hours would be torturous until she finally saw Elizabeth with her own eyes.

CHAPTER 2

W HEN FAITH AWOKE from her restless sleep, she was
still on the airplane. The lady beside her, a blanket
over her shoulders, snored gently. These long transatlantic
flights were rough in the best of times, but Faith was used to
it. She had a couple flights she loved—the Singapore flight
was one of them, along with this Norway flight. She settled
back and smiled when the flight attendant brought her a cup
of coffee. "Thank you," Faith whispered in the silent plane.

"We'll be landing in just under an hour. So you have
time for this."

"Perfect," Faith said with a smile. In fact, it was better
than that, as it meant she'd gotten some sleep. And that was
important. Just as she was about to settle into her laptop, the
flight attendant returned with a full meal.

"You slept through yours."

Realizing she didn't have a clue what she was arriving
into, she pulled her little table toward her and proceeded to
polish off the food. When everything was gone, they were
already on their descent.

The little old lady beside her had trouble waking up. She
kept yawning and covering her mouth. She was smiling—she
was sweet. She leaned over to Faith. "I'll see my grandchil-
dren."

"That'll be fun," Faith returned.

They were about to land. And after that it was the usual chaos of getting off the airplane. The flight attendant let her off first. There were some benefits to being a pilot herself. She raced through the tarmac, into the building and to the other side. She grabbed the first cab and gave him the address for the hospital. In silence he drove her right there. She used a credit card to pay him and stormed inside the hospital.

When the big doors closed behind her, she stopped and stood for a moment. She'd made it. Now the question was, was she in time? Her stomach sick at the thought, she walked over to the reception desk, hoping someone would speak English. But just as she went to ask where her friend was, a voice called out.

"Faith."

She spun to see Mary racing toward her. They hugged, and, when she stepped back slightly, Faith asked, "And?"

Mary smiled. "She's still holding on."

She led Faith down to her sister's side. At the sight of the tubes, bandages and swelling, Faith stopped at the doorway, her heart seizing, her breath catching in the back of her throat.

Mary leaned over and gripped her fingers. "I'm so sorry. I should've warned you."

Faith shook her head. "There is no preparing anyone for this." She took several small steps forward. "Is it safe to hold her hand?"

"You can touch it, just don't lift it."

Faith pulled a chair up close and covered her friend's long fingers with her own. "Elizabeth, can you hear me?"

She tossed a glance at Mary who shook her head. "She's still sedated."

The machines beeped reassuringly at Elizabeth's side. Faith reached her other hand to gently stroke Elizabeth's forearm. And then she talked to her friend in a gentle tone. "Come back to us, Elizabeth. Keep fighting the good fight. You've never been a quitter. I'm so sorry this happened to you."

Faith didn't know how long she had rambled on, but it seemed like the words just tumbled off her lips. She didn't have any rhyme or reason for when one conversation ended and the next started, but it seemed like she was running through their best memories and some of their toughest times.

Finally she fell silent and let her head drop onto the bed beside Elizabeth's prone body. And Faith relaxed. She could feel her best friend's pulse underneath her fingers, and Elizabeth's fingers twitched every once in a while. A couple times Faith thought maybe those movements were in response to her voice, but the doctors who'd been in had assured her it was just nerves twitching. There was nothing reassuring about that.

Then the nurses came around, asking Faith to leave because they had dressings to change. Outside the room Faith walked up and down the hall for a long time. She didn't know what to do with herself. She didn't have a place to stay, and she couldn't even think about leaving Elizabeth. There was no sign of Mary. Faith sat down in one of the chairs in the hallway and scrubbed her face. She needed food. Coffee would be good. Through her fatigue she heard voices.

She looked up at the sound of someone speaking English. And her jaw dropped. The two men she had shared the cab with in her hometown were talking to a doctor. Their conversation was low and urgent. A third man joined them, speaking Norwegian. Finally the doctor walked away, leaving the three men talking together. They were obviously friends.

Given this moment to observe them unaware, she smiled. The one guy was just as she had remembered him gloved hand. She hadn't thought anything about it before, when she had first met him, but now she watched his movements closer. She frowned. That may be a prosthetic hand. She wondered what kind of an accident he had been in to lose his left hand. Her heart immediately went out to him. Maybe it was this hospital environment that had her emotions so raw and easily displayed, but she wouldn't even be here if not for Elizabeth. Faith was sure Elizabeth wouldn't choose to be here either, given that choice.

Curious and wondering about the synchronicity that would have two people from Santa Fe, New Mexico, halfway around the world in the same hospital, she approached and said, "Hi. You guys remember me?"

Two of the men turned to look at her with blank faces, but the one man's face lit up with recognition. "You're the pilot."

She reached out and shook his hand. "I'm Faith Halladay."

"Cade Terence," he said by way of introduction. He motioned to the two men beside him. "Talon was in the cab with us that day we first met. And this is Laszlo. A friend of ours."

"Are you Norwegian?" she asked Laszlo, wondering at the single black glove he wore on his left hand.

He nodded. "My father and brother live here."

"But not you?"

He shrugged. "I was in the US for over a decade. Now I'm not exactly sure where I live."

That surprised her. But she understood in a way. "That makes sense. I've been a pilot long enough that sometimes I'm not sure what country I belong in anymore."

The men nodded in agreement. "That happens when you travel a lot."

"Or when life throws you a curve ball, and everything changes," Talon said.

Cade looked at her. "It doesn't look like you're here for a very nice reason either."

She smiled. "Is that a polite way of saying that I look like crap?"

He shrugged. "You could never look like crap, but it's obvious you're tired and under an emotional strain."

She reached out and gripped his fingers. "I'm sorry. I didn't mean to put you on the spot. The truth is, I flew over because my best friend was in a car accident. She's not expected to make it, and I wanted to get here before she passed."

At the sadness in her voice Cade squeezed her fingers back. "I'm so sorry."

"At least she made it through the night so I could be by her side." Faith tried for a brighter smile. "And every day is a chance for her to fight for the next day." She turned to see Elizabeth's room was still full of doctors and nurses. "They kicked me out. That's when I realized I didn't have a place to go. After landing, I came straight here. I haven't taken a break for coffee or food." She shook her head. "Talk about throwing me a curve ball." She glanced at Laszlo. "I don't suppose you'd take a walk through the cafeteria with me, so I can get a meal?"

He chuckled. "Most people here speak some English. But we should probably grab something to eat too." He glanced at the other two men with an eyebrow raised. They all nodded.

"Why are you guys here?" she asked as Laszlo led them down the hall.

"My father was in a hit-and-run accident a month ago," Laszlo said quietly. "We came back to check on him."

"He's okay though?"

Laszlo's tone deepened as he said, "He survived, if that's what you mean."

She thought about what he'd said. "Right. Nobody is really okay after something like that, are they?"

He nodded.

For whatever reason she didn't seem to want to leave it alone. Maybe it was hearing his father had survived that gave her hope for her own friend. "Is he still in the hospital?

"No, he's home now. We were just checking in with the doctor to see what kind of treatment was available." He opened a large door for her.

She stepped in to see a fairly calm dining room atmosphere, unlike what she would have expected in a North American hospital. Every time she walked into one in the States, it seemed to be noisy with pots and pans clanging and people talking. But then she realized it was close to midnight here.

As a group they walked through the cafeteria. She was happy to hear that, although the languages were not all English, she could make herself understood. At the cash register she pulled out a credit card. "I only have US cash."

Laszlo smiled. "Credit cards work for everything here."

After she paid, she turned around to look for a place to sit. She should have asked the doctors how long they needed before she could return. The men grouped around her and pointed to a table off by the window. She walked over and sat down, surprised and delighted when they joined her. Cade and Talon only had coffee. Laszlo appeared to have a large sandwich with a big chunk of bread on the side.

She smiled. "I didn't see anything like that on the menu board."

He shrugged as he pulled off his glove and laid it beside him. "Some food you have to know to ask for."

She almost missed what he said, her gaze caught on the badly damaged hand. No wonder Laszlo wore a glove. With a mental headshake she focused on her meal. She'd picked up a salad, thinking it was probably safe. But it wouldn't give her a ton of substance. Laszlo reached across and gave her a large portion of his bread. "If you're here, you should at least try the bread. It's a regular food at all meals."

She took a bite, her eyebrows lifting. "This is lovely."

He nodded.

Without worrying about showing her hunger, she wrapped her fingers around her fork and polished off her food. When she pushed away her plate, she said, "I didn't think I'd be able to eat."

"Emotional shocks are like that," Cade said. "You're much better off to force yourself to eat and to give your stomach something other than itself to work on."

She winced at the thought. The whole time she'd been eating, he'd been on the phone. She wasn't sure exactly what was going on, but obviously this trip wasn't a holiday for him. Then again, if he had his own business, he might be able to work from anywhere. "Working vacation?"

His lips twitched. "Something like that." He pulled out a card and wrote something on it. He pushed it toward her. "My number, in case you need us."

Surprised and touched, she accepted it with a thank-you. She glanced up at them and said, "If you find out anything, hear anything about Elizabeth, can you tell me please? I can't understand any of the conversations going on around me, and I know some of it is about her."

"What's your number?" Cade asked. "And no promises, but, if we get wind of anything, we'll be happy to pass the information on."

Pleased, she gave him her number.

"You really shouldn't be so open about that," Cade scolded her gently. "We could be serial killers."

She rolled her eyes. "In that case, lose my number," she joked. "Still, it's not something I do lightly. Just goes to show the depth of my concern for Elizabeth."

The men exchanged glances but didn't elaborate.

These men were the types to have secrets. Not that that was a bad thing. She could use a little more privacy sometimes in her life too. She glanced at her watch and realized she'd been away from Elizabeth's room for close to an hour. "I'll head back again." She smiled. "Thanks for the company and the assistance." She collected her dishes, turned and added them to other dirty dishes on a table beside the kitchen's Employees Only door.

With a last glance back at the men, whose heads were bent over Cade's cell phone, she made her way to Elizabeth's room.

The last nurse was just leaving. She held the door open and said, "No change."

Grateful to hear English, yet sad at the news but not ready to give up yet, Faith sat down and gently covered Elizabeth's hand. "Elizabeth, I'm back."

CADE SAID, "ERICK just texted that he received the accident reports for your father."

"How did he get that so fast?" Laszlo shook his head. "The doctor downstairs just refused to give it to us, if you remember."

"He said we weren't entitled to it or something along those lines."

"Same diff," Laszlo snorted.

"He's also got his brother's and Badger's parents' reports, and he has my sister's report. Anybody hear from Geir yet?"

"No. What about Erick? Has he spoken to Geir?" Talon asked.

"I'll ask him." Cade sent a text. The response was almost instant. "He says no."

"And did anybody reach Jager yet?" Laszlo added.

"Erick is on that. He has what he has, and Tesla has agreed to start extrapolating some of the data."

"Not sure Stone isn't already on it too," Talon said. "Between those two, I'd be surprised if anybody manages to pull a fast one on us again."

"Why did it take us two years to figure this out?" Cade asked them.

"Because, in those two years," Laszlo said, "most of us were recuperating, and most of these accidents hadn't happened. Neither did we all sit down and compare notes. We also don't know that we've got anything figured out yet either. It's just an awful lot of disturbing coincidences."

Talon laughed. "You know exactly how I feel about that."

Laszlo checked his watch. "Okay, the specialist can see

us now."

They got up and walked to a different part of the hospital. Cade knocked on the specialist's door and entered with Talon and Laszlo following. The doctor looked up and smiled, then reached across the desk and shook hands with all three. Cade listened as the Norwegian flowed thick and fast around the room. And just as abruptly as it started, it ended. The men shook hands again, and Laszlo turned to motion them out of the room. In the hall he said, "Only lifesaving treatments were done at the time, but, now that my father is in a little better shape, the doctor wants to see him again. So I'll take that as a good sign."

"Is it hard for your father to get around?"

"It is. I think I'll hire somebody to stay with him and my brother."

The men studied Laszlo's face. "Are you sure you don't want to go home and take care of that yourself?"

He shook his head. "No. I'm just not sure who to hire."

"Mason or Levi might have an idea."

Laszlo looked at him in surprise. "Why them?"

"They have worldwide contacts. What you really need is somebody who'll drive them back and forth, plus do the shopping, cooking, things like that, but can also be a guard," Talon said. "Your father is the only one who survived these attacks."

Laszlo's face darkened. "I can send Levi a text." He stopped and frowned. "Or Bullard. Maybe he has somebody closer."

Cade stared at him. "I know the name, but I don't know the man."

Talon smiled. "Well, you'd certainly never forget him if you did meet him. He has a place similar to Levi's but fancier and in Africa. Dave works for him, managing the estate, like Alfred at Levi's."

"You think they might know somebody?"

"It can't hurt to ask."

"I suggest we toss this onto Erick's plate and see if he can find somebody suitable."

"Preferably somebody already in Europe—or, even better, in the Scandinavian area."

"As long as he can be here in the next few days, that will be good enough."

As they walked outside the hospital, Laszlo lifted his keys to pop open the car locks. Cade got into the back and pulled out his phone. "I'll get a hold of someone. Maybe Levi is the better one in all this. He can talk to Bullard, see if he can shake somebody loose." He sent a text to Erick, surprised when a response came back almost immediately. "Erick is on it."

"Perfect," Laszlo said. "We're almost there."

When Cade turned to look around, he realized they were heading out into the country. "I thought you guys lived in town?"

"Not for a long time," Laszlo said. "My dad's always been a bit of a loner. And, after my mom passed away, he wanted to get farther away from people."

"Something we all understand," Talon said. "We've seen enough of the world. It's nice to have open space."

Laszlo took a right turn and then a left turn onto a long driveway. Cade studied the area with interest. Rolling hills and trees, lots of rock. He smiled. "What are the winters like?"

"Well, let's just say it's a real winter here," Laszlo said drily.

At the front of a house that looked like a sprawling bungalow, he hopped out, and the others followed suit. Cade motioned toward the trunk. "If we're staying here too, want to get our bags out?"

"Let's see how things are first," Laszlo said. He pocketed the keys. "We can always come back and grab our bags."

Interested to meet Laszlo's family, they walked inside to find no one at home.

Cade glanced at his friend. "Where are they?"

Laszlo rolled his eyes. "They'll be in the back."

He walked through the main part of the house to another section where, even though it was the middle of summer, a roaring fire blazed in the fireplace, and two men sat on the couch with what looked like an alcoholic drink similar to a beer in front of each of them, watching a sports game on TV. Laszlo stepped in front of the men, and both men cried out in surprise. He stopped them both from their struggles to stand up, leaning over and giving each a hug.

He put the TV on Pause and said, "I'm here with a couple friends." He motioned the two men over, and Cade stepped up to shake Laszlo's father's hand.

Laszlo said, "This is Henry. Or at least a close-enough form of my father's name that you can use."

They shook hands.

"And this is my brother, Jair."

Cade shook his hand and smiled at the man who looked similar enough to Laszlo to recognize the family resemblance. But whereas Laszlo glowed with health and vitality, Jair looked to be on the sinking end of life. And yet he was the younger brother, as far as Cade knew. He glanced at Laszlo's father to see he was not in much better shape.

"I'm happy to finally meet Laszlo's family," Cade said

quietly. The two men looked at each other.

Laszlo said with a smile, "Although English is spoken in many parts of the world, neither of these two understand it." He quickly translated, and the men beamed and nodded.

They spoke for a few more minutes, and then Laszlo turned the TV back on and ushered Cade and Talon out into the other part of the house. "We'll stay here for the next couple days, until we get somebody to help them. In the meantime, they haven't eaten."

"Is that our job too?" Cade joked. It made sense if mobility and lack of energy were issues. And he was no slouch in the kitchen.

"It is now." Laszlo walked into the kitchen, opened the fridge and cupboards, checking each. "And, of course, they haven't shopped."

"I gather they struggle to get through the day," Cade said. "Do we need to head into town and fill up the cupboards?"

"We've got enough for tonight," Laszlo said. "But it won't be fancy." He went to the freezer and pulled out the ground meat. "I can throw something together. But we'll have to do a major shopping trip tomorrow."

Cade stepped in to help, knowing his friend was perturbed at his family's inability to look after themselves, even when it came to the basics. "The problem with two injured people is they tend to not want to make the effort for themselves and don't want to ask the other to make the effort for them either because they both are in rough shape."

Laszlo nodded, taking off his glove and placing it on the side. Then started to unwrap the meat. "That's why I need somebody else here. I left them food, but they've eaten everything that was easy to access and walked away from anything harder."

"And we've all done the same thing many times over these last couple years. Not to worry. We'll get them some help."

Pitching in together, the three of them produced a meal, and very quickly Laszlo served up two large bowls to take to his brother and father.

Cade sat at the kitchen counter, and his phone pinged. He had turned it off so he could eat and then realized he didn't dare take the chance of missing an email with these attacks on their families. With Talon behind him watching, he flicked through all the messages. "Things are blowing up."

"In what way?"

"Erick said Tesla managed to get into the bug we left at the arms dealer."

Talon straightened. "She managed to what?"

Cade nodded. "He's told somebody we were looking for the purchaser of those two land mines."

"He didn't say it in English surely?"

"No, she ran it through a translator." Cade read on. "The buyer wanted to know exactly who was asking. When our gun supplier told him, apparently he started to laugh."

At that, Talon and Cade stared at each other. "He knows us," they said in unison.

CHAPTER 3

FAITH WOKE UP with a start. The steady beep of the machines reassured her that Elizabeth was still alive. The room was dark except for the small light over the head of the bed. Faith wasn't sure what woke her, but, as she straightened, she groaned. The back of her neck had kinked from lying with her head on Elizabeth's bed. Definitely not the most comfortable sleeping position. She sat up and leaned back slowly, reaching to massage her shoulders and neck. Realizing that wouldn't be enough, she stood and stretched to the floor and then to the ceiling.

The whole time there was no sign of any change in Elizabeth. Her body didn't appear to have shifted at all since Faith had last looked. She leaned over and kissed her friend gently on the cheek. "If you're in there, Elizabeth, just heal, sweetie. Take your time. Don't answer. Don't respond. Just put all your energy into healing. Stay alive. The doctors don't know everything. Miracles happen, and you've always been my miracle."

Faith settled again in her chair, picked up her laptop and checked the time. Her emails were ringing softly as they were downloaded. It was just after six in the morning. She suspected the nurses would be in soon, and she'd take that time to grab some food and coffee. She'd love a shower, but that didn't seem to be in the offing. She didn't know if this hospital had any facilities for long-term guests like that.

She had often wondered why something like that wasn't available the world over, especially at the major hospitals or the ones with cancer specialties. Surely those medical facilities drew in tons of patients and their family members from all over the planet. People came to look after their loved ones or to be with them, and yet there was rarely any place for them to go but a hotel, which meant leaving the people they cared about in the time of these crises. Not a good solution.

Her instincts were right on; the nurses opened the door and stepped in less than five minutes later. They looked at her and smiled. "You're awake. Did you sleep all night?"

Faith shook her head. "No, I dozed off and on, but there's been no change in her condition."

The nurse nodded and checked on Elizabeth. "That's not necessarily a bad thing. We didn't expect her to last this long. Every day she survives gives us that extra bit of hope."

"Was the head injury enough to cause brain damage?" Faith asked, as that had been one of the biggest fears she'd held.

The nurse shook her head. "No. We've been keeping a close eye on it. But the swelling of the brain hasn't been bad enough to even warrant surgery. She just needs time to heal. The internal bleeding was severe. We pumped a lot of blood in, but it seemed like we were still losing her. When the organs start failing, there's not much we can do. She's holding though, and that's what's important."

Faith smiled down at her friend. "Hear that, Elizabeth? Every day you're alive is a really good sign. So you stick around and keep fighting. Do you hear me?"

Of course there was no answer.

The nurse reached out a gentle hand to pat Faith's shoulder. "Go walk around a little bit. Go to the cafeteria. Pick up some coffee, maybe some breakfast. The doctor won't be here for a bit, but I need to check her over."

Faith nodded. "I was just thinking the same. I should have grabbed a hotel. But I don't want to leave her side."

"Good. She's hung on so far."

"Where is her family?"

The nurse gave her a patient look. "The family finds it difficult to see Elizabeth at this stage. Death is painful for many people."

"She's not dead yet though," Faith protested. "She deserves every chance we can give her."

"Which is why I'm letting you stay here. I wouldn't have given her much chance of survival before you arrived, but now ..." She tilted her head as she considered her patient with a curious look. "She seems a little more stable. Not in so much pain. Definitely calmer now."

Faith would like to think she'd had something to do with that. She returned her laptop to her large bag, pointing at her other luggage. "Is it okay if I leave my carry-on bag here?"

The nurse nodded. "No problem at all."

She picked up her large purse and headed downstairs.

The cafeteria was always open, and, at this hour, it was calm and quiet. That suited her. She walked around to find some food. She stuck to something simple again, not being much of a world traveler in terms of food adventures, but scrambled eggs and toast were pretty universal.

With her tray full she sat down and pulled out her laptop. She had to wonder at seeing Cade here. How terrible for Laszlo that his father had been in a hit-and-run. She hoped the police found whoever did it. She wasn't sure she understood the details of Elizabeth's accident. But she'd been driving at the time, so it might just have been bad road conditions.

Faith stared out the window at the bright sun breaking free of the horizon. She couldn't imagine knowing somebody had hit her father, then drove away to avoid being caught.

Elizabeth was a schoolteacher. She adored all children from infants up. Yet Faith wasn't sure she wanted any children. She'd been an only child, and, although she'd hated that, her mother had been very quick to cling and to become almost a child herself. As far as Faith was concerned, she was mothering her mother already. The thought of starting all over again with a newborn—or even a two-year-old—was daunting.

Of course she didn't have a partner in her life either, and maybe that would change her mind. Particularly if he wanted a family. There was just no way to know. She'd gone into flying because of her love of planes. She'd always been addicted. Her mother had fought her strenuously.

So, when she finally got her first job as a commercial airline pilot, making terrible money, her mother had burst into tears. Now seven years later, her mother had come to terms with it but still wasn't happy. And, of course, she didn't see Faith as much as she wanted to, because Faith was, for a long time, volunteering for as many flights as she could. The number of hours she was allowed to work a week was limited, but, anytime she could get on a route, she took it. She imagined, if she had had the same love of driving, she'd be a nomad wandering the world. Having her own plane was not in the cards. That was an expense she could ill afford. And wasn't sure she wanted one. Even a small one.

She really enjoyed the big jets. A tiny twin-engine turboprop two-seater would feel like a toy. It appealed to a lot of pilots. She'd seen many end up owning one. Particularly when they retired, and again maybe that would change for her down the road, but it wasn't for her now.

"Elizabeth, we were supposed to travel. What happened to that? I have all these flyer points, free flights, and I could never get you to come with me," she murmured.

Most of the time Elizabeth was busy volunteering with other children, the homeless, the helpless, those who just needed a hug. Elizabeth was an eternal mother figure, partially because she knew she could never have children of her own. This accident certainly wouldn't have helped that prognosis either.

Faith sat at the table all alone, going through her emails. She'd asked for compassionate leave from her job, and they'd cleared her for one week. It wasn't technically a family member, but it was a best friend. And Faith had been more than prepared to beg or plead to get the time off. She'd stepped up every time anybody else needed somebody's shift covered. And thankfully others were stepping up to cover hers. By the time she finished going through her emails, had eaten her breakfast and sat back with a second cup of coffee, she could think a little clearer.

How long was it feasible to stay with Elizabeth? To even contemplate seven days was a joy because it meant Elizabeth would still be alive. Faith hoped the doctors would have a better idea within at least forty-eight hours.

She looked up to see the doctor Cade had spoken with yesterday. He glanced her way, smiled and kept going. Then she had that air of desolation and sadness around her. Not exactly something anybody wanted to spend time with.

Her phone buzzed. She checked the message coming through.

Did you grab a hotel last night? Did you get any rest?

She smiled in surprise. She hadn't expected Cade to remember who she was or even why she was here. And certainly she hadn't expected him to send her a message just to check on her. She had no idea what he was up to here in Norway, although, with the hit-and-run, chances were he and his two friends were looking for details. They looked like those kinds of guys.

She frowned as she stared at the message. Instinctively her fingers went to tap out a message in response. **No, stayed at the hospital overnight. Just having a meal at the cafeteria now.** And she wasn't sure whether it was good manners or the fact that he'd been kind enough to reach out, but she typed back, **Did you?**

The response was immediate, as if he had been sitting right there, waiting to hear from her. **Went to Laszlo's for the night. Slept fine. It's a new day.**

It's a new day, and Elizabeth is still alive. I'll take it. And she smiled. Just reconnecting with somebody was huge. She wasn't exactly sure where Elizabeth's sister, Mary, was; and a part of Faith had wondered at Elizabeth's sister's ability to leave the hospital for so long a period of time. But maybe Mary had other responsibilities. Faith knew a lot about Elizabeth's mother, and the last time Faith and Elizabeth had spoken, Faith had assumed nothing had really changed in Elizabeth's world. And maybe Mary had gone home out of exhaustion and just slept, completely forgetting Faith was here. Or maybe remembering that Faith was here for her sister let Mary off the hook for a bit.

Also Faith wasn't Mary's responsibility. Faith was an adult with the means to take care of herself. She got up and took her tray of dirty dishes over to the others atop the table near the kitchen. She returned to her table, packed up her laptop, and, as she went to put her phone in her purse, she got another message from Cade.

What happened to your friend? Was it an accident?

She stared at that and wondered. She knew his suspicions were probably coming from Laszlo's father's hit-and-run. **I believe so. I haven't gotten any details yet.**

Hopefully the police know about it.

Faith wondered about that. Back in Elizabeth's hospital room, the nurses had left. Faith took her seat, opened up her laptop and quickly sent Mary an email. **Elizabeth had a good night. She's still holding her own.** Faith thought for a moment and then added, **Mary, do you have the details on Elizabeth's accident? Every day is a gift. I'd like to see the police report if possible.** And then, without giving herself a chance to question why, she hit Send.

CADE POCKETED HIS cell phone and said, "I just heard back from Faith. Her friend is still alive. So that's good news. She doesn't have any details about that accident."

Laszlo nodded. "Not everybody's accident will be deliberate."

"Which, of course, means it wasn't an accident," Talon interjected. "What's on tap for today?"

"I want to go to the accident site," Laszlo said abruptly. "I was there once before, when I first arrived. But I was pretty busy looking after my father. I want to go back and walk the area."

"There's not likely to be anything to see."

Laszlo nodded. "But I want to see it again. With fresh eyes. With our new perspective."

They got in the car and headed out within minutes. The accident spot was only a few miles away. They got out and Laszlo explained what had happened. "He was walking on the right side of the shoulder."

"And it was dark?"

"Half dark. It was dusky. But it was also the normal time that he always went for a walk every night."

"So a routine anybody would know after a few days," Cade said.

Laszlo nodded, his tone turned grim. "Exactly."

The men walked a mile down this strip, then back on the other side. Cade could see it happening. Old man unaware of anything but whatever he was thinking about at the moment, following a routine he had perfected over the years. It was a comfort to have this routine. It also helped his digestive system, and the dogs, almost as old as he was, were content to walk at his side. Odd that the dogs hadn't been hit. But their instincts to get out of danger were better and faster than humans' gut reactions.

Cade turned to Laszlo. "Does your father have a hearing aid? Would he have heard the vehicle?"

"He has a hearing aid. I don't know if he was wearing it that night. If he was, he would have heard the vehicle, but he would not have expected it to be a problem."

"And we don't know if he lunged off to the side to get away or whether he was struck down where he stood?" Talon asked. "They should be able to tell that much from his injuries."

"He was struck down from the back."

Cade winced. "So he really didn't see it coming."

"No, and he can't tell me anything about the accident. He said he was walking, and, the next thing he knew, he was waking up in the hospital."

"To be expected. Even if there wasn't any memory loss associated with the trauma, a blow like that would have hit him and knocked him unconscious almost immediately."

There was nothing to see at the accident site. The guys were expecting that, but all were disappointed nonetheless. It was a completely straight stretch of road with a nice wide shoulder. The vehicle would have had no trouble avoiding the old man. "Weather conditions? Road conditions?" Talon asked.

"Dry, clear."

The three men exchanged glances.

"So the driver comes along," Cade theorizes, "swerves to the side, hits your father and carries on. Was it deliberate? Was the driver drunk? On drugs? Innocently mixing the wrong prescription medications? Hell, it could have been someone texting on their damn phone while driving. Or maybe he was reaching for something on the floor of the vehicle that he'd accidently dropped, and it really was an accident? And he left in a panic at what he had done? Or was he out for a joyride and thought, out of the blue, he would just kill somebody?" Cade asked. Unfortunately any and all scenarios were possible. "No witnesses?" Cade turned to look around at the nearby landscape. "There doesn't appear to be any other houses around here."

"There aren't," Laszlo said. "This is a very isolated country area. All the properties are large with long driveways leading to houses well set back from the roads. Somebody might have seen the vehicle come down the road if they were watching out a window, but they wouldn't have necessarily seen if the vehicle hit somebody. They might have seen if the vehicle stopped, however," he said pensively. Turning to face Cade and Talon, he said, "We should do a door-to-door canvas. Talk to the neighbors around here. Who knows? Maybe another neighbor takes a walk at the same time at night, and they may have crossed paths with my father from time to time."

Cade nodded, his mouth twisted, but he didn't say anything.

Laszlo continued. "At the very least we should speak to these closest neighbors. They might be able to tell us something."

"But not much." Cade motioned at the driveway opposite where the accident had occurred, with the house not visible from the road. "We should check it out though."

The three men got back in the vehicle and drove down the long driveway. They hopped out in front of the large farmhouse-looking building. Talon waited at the vehicle, while Cade and Laszlo walked up to the front door. Laszlo knocked and then called out.

A woman opened the door.

He spoke to her quickly, and the conversation was fluid in a back-and-forth exchange. But almost immediately she shook her head, and Cade realized that, of course, she hadn't seen anything. If she had, her eyes, rheumy and slightly opaque, wouldn't have seen clearly.

When Laszlo was done, he smiled and motioned for Cade to leave with him. "She saw a vehicle that night, and she did see it slow down. Then it left. She only heard about the accident afterward. She didn't realize that was probably the vehicle that hit my father. She did tell the police, however, but there was nothing she could give in the way of more information or details."

Cade nodded. "It's what I expected."

On that note they got back into their vehicle and drove to the main road. Laszlo sat there with the engine running. "I want to go to the police station. I've seen a police report, but I want to know if there are any updates."

They followed him into the police station ten minutes later. The hospital wasn't very far away. Cade could see it at the end of the block. Knowing he wouldn't be any help at the police station, he said to Laszlo, "I'll walk over and talk to Faith. When you're done here, come over."

Laszlo nodded. "I can do that. I also want to talk to the doctor. Again."

He didn't explain why, and Cade didn't need details. If it had been his father, he'd have done anything to get answers. But the problem was, at some point, there just weren't answers to find. Somebody hit an old man on the side of the road. And then that person hadn't called for help, just had taken off. The chance of finding out who it was—when there were no witnesses, no forensic evidence—was pretty slim. It didn't change the fact that, as far as Cade was concerned, this was likely a targeted hit. The question now was, did the driver care that his attempted murder was just that and not a completed job? Cade thought about saying something to Laszlo, but he'd already entered the police station.

Talon walked with Cade to the hospital. "What are you thinking about?"

"I'm wondering," Cade said, "if this attempted murder is classified as a failure, will this guy come back? And how is he following up on his hit?"

"I was considering the same thing," Talon said. "But we already brought it up. Hence the need for a bodyguard who could care for Laszlo's family."

"Yet it's been a month. So why bother?" Cade shrugged. "Wouldn't the guy have finished off Henry by now if that was his original intention?"

"What's the rush?" Talon stated. "Especially if these are intended to be *accidents*. Not to mention Henry is seventy-four years old. He could still die without this asshole taking any more action. If this is the same person systematically taking out all our family members, he's done it in his own good time. From as early as six months after the land mine hit our military unit to just one month ago here in Norway. That spans over seventeen months. This guy is working from whatever pattern or order that matters to him. And that could be just convenience, especially if he's nowhere close to Norway again."

"Exactly," Cade said. "But how would we know?"

"If he's not a local, he'll have a rental vehicle. And he'll need a place to stay."

"This is a small town," Cade added. "There are only two hotels and only one rental agency."

"Sure, but we know you can do a one-way drop-off. Or he could have picked up a car from whatever city he flew into, rented it for a couple days and returned it."

"And that'll mean thousands of vehicles to check," Cade said, sighing. "But the police said the injuries were consistent with an SUV, not a truck. And Henry's doctor confirmed that. Given how quickly info can be pulled from databases, I'm pretty sure a couple phone calls would offer us a bunch of names."

"Does that help? He likely used a fake name," Talon pointed out.

"True." Cade's mind churned on how to find more information as to who could have done this. "What if the guy isn't local and hasn't returned to finish the job because he's not up to date. *Yet.* He'd have to know that he botched the job to begin with. So he'd check out the obits. Not finding Henry's name in the online newspapers, he could have called the hospital—this one," Cade said, pointing at the building now in front of them, "asking to check on the status of his *friend*." He raised his eyebrows as he looked at Talon. "Would he have had the balls to call the police for an update?"

"I can see calling the hospital but the police would raise alarms."

They entered the hospital and headed to the hospital room where they'd seen Faith. They glanced through the window in the door and saw her sitting in a chair, staring out the bedroom window. Cade gently opened the door and whispered, "Faith?"

He watched the surprise cross her face. She stood, putting down the laptop and stepped out of the room with him.

"Hi," she said with a smile.

He put his arms around her, giving her a hug. She probably had no idea how absolutely devastated she looked. But, when she clung in his arms for longer than necessary, he realized he was right to do what he'd done. He wasn't an impetuous person, but she needed a friend right now.

Talon raised an eyebrow at him.

But Cade ignored him and just held her close.

When she stepped back, she wiped a tear from her eye. "Thank you. I don't really know you, but I needed that," she said on a broken laugh.

"How's your friend?" he asked, deliberately ignoring her comment and giving her space.

"No change. I keep hoping for some sign of consciousness, but ..."

"She probably can't surface right now," Talon said. "I'd assume the doctors are keeping her sedated, letting her body heal as much as it can."

She turned to face him, a sad smile on her face. "Or because they're expecting her to just pass and want to make it as painless as possible."

Cade reached out and gently squeezed her shoulder. "Keep hoping. We've seen a lot of miracles."

Her smile brightened. "Me too. That's what I keep telling Elizabeth. *Just keep fighting. And I'll be here.*"

"You had no problem getting out of work?"

"No, I got somebody to cover my first shift, and now I've been given a week off for compassionate leave."

"Good. But you can't just stay here the whole time."

"I was thinking that maybe later today I'd find a hotel and crash for the night."

Just then the doctor walked in. The nurse approached and said, "You have to stay outside for a little while."

Watching the mix of expressions on Faith's face, Cade asked the nurse, "Can we collect her luggage? We'll find her a hotel."

Faith looked at him in surprise. But he had already gone inside, picked up her belongings and brought them out to her. "Thank you." Faith looked at Talon and Cade. "You guys don't have to do this. I'm sure there's one around the corner."

"Let's go see," Cade said.

Talon walked on the other side of her. She looked up at the two of them. "Are you both here to find out about your friend's father's accident?"

Talon stiffened and glanced at her cautiously. "It's certainly one thing we're looking into."

"I haven't had a chance to talk to the police about Elizabeth's accident," Faith said. "I did ask her sister, but I didn't get an answer yet."

"Was Elizabeth driving?"

"I believe so, but I'm not sure about that. I really don't know any details." Outside, she'd stopped on the front step, the two men stopping beside her.

Cade watched as she took several deep bracing gulps of air. He could see the fatigue pulling on her cheeks and the tired droop to her eyes. He slipped her arm through his. "C'mon. Let's get you a hotel room, a place to crash for a few hours. You can come back and see Elizabeth then."

She shook her head. "She might not live that long," she said in a stark tone.

"If that's the case, there's nothing you can do for her. But what we don't want is to have you end up in a hospital bed beside her."

She shot him a startled look. "Do I look that bad?"

He grinned. "Fishing for compliments? That's a good sign."

She rolled her eyes at him.

He ushered her toward the front doors of a hotel—right across the street on the same block. She stopped and looked up at the sign. "How did you even know this was a hotel?"

He chuckled. "I checked Google Maps. And this is the closest one. You can walk this block easily back and forth to see your friend."

Inside he waited for her to register. It was really early in the day, compared to what was check-out time, but they did have empty rooms, so they let her get in. Particularly after he explained what was going on.

His phone rang just then. Laszlo's number showed on his screen. Cade explained where they were, which was just across the street from the police station. Moments later Laszlo walked in behind them. He spoke to the hotel manager and got Faith's room changed to one on the front of the street, so she could see out. They escorted her to her room and left her there. She smiled as she closed the door, whispering, "Thank you."

Cade nodded. As he turned to walk away, he added, "Sleep well."

Laszlo and Talon stared at him. He shrugged, then walked toward the stairs and back down to the front reception. "She's a fellow countrywoman. I couldn't just leave her feeling lost."

The others were silent.

"Did you know her before?" Laszlo asked.

Talon spoke up. "We shared a cab with her when we came back from Kabul."

Laszlo's face cleared. "*Aah*. That explains that."

"Explains what?" Cade asked in irritation. This was no big deal. He was just helping her get a room so she didn't kill herself waiting for her friend to wake up or to die. "What did the police say?"

Laszlo held up copies of the accident report. "I've got printed copies this time. They have nothing new to add." He glanced around. "I need something to eat. There's a good café around the corner or so. Let's go there, and I can give you a quick overview."

They walked outside and down several blocks before they stepped into a small family-looking restaurant. Laszlo ordered coffee and breakfast for all three of them.

As he sat down, Cade held out his hand. "Let me see." The paperwork was handed over, and he held it so both he and Talon could take a look. Laszlo gave them the gist of the report. Cade turned the page only to realize the second page was almost blank. "Nothing else?"

Laszlo shot him a grim look. "No, nothing else."

Talon said, "Cade and I discussed checking out rental vehicles. If somebody targeted us and wasn't a local, they would need a vehicle. Chances are he flew in, rented an SUV for potentially one or two days, maybe longer in order to get an idea of your father's routine, did the job and then flew out."

Laszlo nodded. "I did check with the neighbors to see if there'd been any strangers hanging around. They all said no. At least none they knew of. Nobody had spoken to them about my father's accident."

Talon frowned. "Not good police work. But, good to know, because that was another option."

"It shouldn't be too hard to get a list of names who rented an SUV."

"No. Not with Ice and Stone at our disposal."

"Plus we need further information off the doctor's report. Or maybe you already know. How tall is your father and where are the actual points of impact?"

Laszlo's gaze lit up at something concrete to determine. "But, just because the police suspect it was an SUV, should we get a forensic specialist?" He stared at Cade, then Talon. "After all, the police hadn't even spent the time to talk to the neighbors. They've got this sealed up as a hit-and-run with no witnesses. End of story. Case closed."

The next fifteen minutes followed a discussion on the height of bumpers on trucks versus SUVs versus cars.

"Of course, this is a rough science, but the best guess would be an SUV," Cade said after their discussion. "So I suggest we get a list of all rental vehicles and check that with flights, potentially see if anybody saw that vehicle here. And ... he had to fuel up somewhere." He watched as Laszlo made notes. "One more thing. Talon and I were tossing around the idea that an out-of-town hired gunman may not know that his first hit wasn't terminal. If our guy is not local, then he'd have to speak to the doctor or the police. What do you think?"

"The detective did tell me that, if we found out anything, to let him know."

"Are all incoming phone calls to the police recorded here? Can he get that information for us though? You think he's willing?"

Laszlo nodded. "He's a friend of my brother's." He picked up his phone and pulled out a card from his pocket. He dialed the detective.

Cade sat back as their breakfasts arrived. He couldn't understand most of Laszlo's conversation anyway. But, as plate after plate after plate—all heaped full of food—were placed on the table, he could feel his stomach growling with joy. He looked at Talon, smiling. "At least they know how to eat over here."

Talon laughed as he picked up a slab of bread and took a bite. "They do indeed."

CHAPTER 4

FAITH WALKED INTO the hotel room, loving the homey coziness of a room that came with an armchair, a small couch, and a large queen-size bed with comforters that poofed up over the bed. Exhausted, she changed into simple panties and a cami, all set to crawl under the covers. She probably should have told Mary what she was doing and where she'd gone, but it was beyond her at the moment. She was just too tired.

Hours later she was feeling, although not fully rested, at least better. Her brain was less foggy, her mind more at peace. She still felt terribly guilty about leaving Elizabeth but knew she could really do nothing that would keep Elizabeth on this planet if Faith had stayed those extra six hours. On the other hand, with more energy, Faith should return and talk to Elizabeth, convincing her with more vigor to fight for her life.

Faith checked her clock and decided that a ten-minute shower wouldn't change anything. She walked into the quaint bathroom, loving everything about it, including the claw-foot tub. She stepped in, pulling the curtain around her. She took a long moment to shampoo her short brunette curls with the handheld sprayer. She'd had her hair cut in a bob about two weeks ago and was still figuring out if she liked the look or not. It was easy to handle, and that was a big plus. After shampooing, she'd put on conditioner and left it in for a few minutes, while she scrubbed the rest of her body down. And she scrubbed hard.

Invigorated when she was done, she stepped out of the tub and wrapped herself in the soft towels. With one twisted around her hair and another around her torso, she walked back into the bedroom and pulled out clean clothes. Her hair would have to dry naturally, since she didn't want to take the time and didn't have the inclination to blow dry it. Dressed, she walked back downstairs, smiled at the woman in the reception area and stepped outside.

It was midafternoon—maybe late afternoon according to where the sun was. She walked the block to the hospital and stepped inside. Hungry but not wanting to waste too much time, she walked through the cafeteria and picked up some food to go, which included coffee, muffins and a sandwich. At the last moment she grabbed a piece of fruit and put it with her purchases.

Armed for the next few hours, she slowly walked back to Elizabeth's room. Without a phone call to let her know what Elizabeth's state was, Faith had no way to know if the news would be good or bad.

As she walked past a hallway, she saw Cade. He was talking to a different man, his two friends with him. She frowned at him. He flashed her a bright smile and said, "You look much better."

She stepped back slightly. "I didn't mean to disturb you. I'm just on my way back to Elizabeth."

Cade nodded toward Laszlo who was talking in Norwegian to the new man in a lab coat. "We're just getting more details as far as injuries."

"Ouch," she said brightly. "I'll leave you to it then." And

she quickly walked down the hall to Elizabeth's door, which was closed. Shuffling the food in her hand, she slowly opened it, petrified of what she might see on the inside. But, to her relief, she heard the machines humming and beeping away in a reassuring rhythm. She smiled and stepped in farther.

"Elizabeth, I'm back." She walked over to the windowsill, laid down her food and drinks, and took off her coat. She put it around the back side of the chair and walked toward Elizabeth. She gently stroked her fingers along Elizabeth's arm. Unable to help herself, Faith bent over and kissed her friend on the cheek. "Any time you want to wake up, I'll be happy."

And yet there was no noticeable change in her best friend. With a sad sigh Faith sat down and ate her lunch, though it was more an early dinner at this point. As she sat here, she realized she'd left the door open. Maybe that was a good thing. Maybe some stimulation would help Elizabeth come back out of whatever coma she was in. And though part of Faith knew there was no way Elizabeth could wake up if the doctors had drugged her asleep, she hoped her friend was aware on a subconscious level that Faith was here with her.

While she munched on her sandwich, Faith could hear footsteps in the hallway. She recognized Cade's voice. And Talon's. They were discussing how the information from the accident report apparently coincided with their belief an SUV had run down Laszlo's father.

As she listened, she heard, "We just got the list of SUVs that were rented. But there were 125 of them." That was Talon speaking.

She no longer heard their footsteps. They must have

stopped somewhere near Elizabeth's room in the hallway outside, since Faith could hear them clearly still.

"I guess we're lucky it's not New York," Cade said. "It could be ten times that number."

"Then we narrowed it down to single males and to those who had a designated drop-off at the airport," Talon continued.

Cade laughed. "That's good thinking. And how many does that leave us with?"

"Forty-two."

"That's reasonable."

"Not necessarily. Out of those there are only four color combinations for SUVs."

"Sure," Cade added. "That'll be silver, blue, black and white."

"One has a fancy name, some kind of muted gray."

"Silver then," Cade said with a snort. "They keep coming up with all these new color names as a marketing ploy. But let's get real. Gray is gray, and silver is silver."

Faith nodded. She'd found something similar herself with cars she'd been looking at.

Cade continued to talk. "We need pictures of the models rented and then to visit each of the gas stations close to where Henry was hit. See if anybody there recognizes the SUV."

"Agreed," Talon said. "The other thing to note is, we had cut more out of the original number based on too much or too little mileage per rental. Those that had too many miles and a longer rental period, we took off the list," Talon explained. "Like someone road-tripping through Scandinavia. Plus those that incurred almost no miles, we took off the list."

"Oh, I guess you considered that Henry's place is a drive from here," Cade mentioned. "And, of course, whether it was a straight trip there and back again, isn't likely. Our hired gun would go a couple times to see what the old man's routine was."

"Exactly. And that cut the number down to twenty-one."

"All colors again?" Cade asked.

"Two colors. Black and silver."

"Any SUVs with smoked or privacy windows?" Cade asked.

Talon chuckled. "We're ahead of you. That dropped us down to seven."

Faith sat in amazement as they narrowed down the vehicles. That number was doable to research.

"Anything else from that?" Cade asked.

"Yes, we checked all seven names. That was, Stone and Ice checked. Of all seven names two were fraudulent."

"So those are the two we want to go after."

"One of them had Mouse as a middle name."

She frowned. Why the hell would somebody have an animal, especially a rodent, as a middle name?

Cade's voice turned hard as he snapped, "Him first."

"Exactly."

"Do we have a picture ID?"

"No, but we do have a license plate, and there are city cameras."

Cade whistled long and clear. "Do we get to view the cameras, or does this fall to the detective to go through?"

"I haven't approached him yet. I figured as soon as Laszlo was done with this doctor, we could walk over to the detective's office and present this information and see if he can help us pull some cameras and maybe get a face off one of them."

"Then I suggest we go there right now. Let's snag Laszlo away from his conversation that's likely to never end, considering it's his family's health they're discussing. Either he comes with us, or we'll go without him."

"We'll need Laszlo for that. Remember the detective is his brother's friend."

Faith finished her sandwich as the men walked away. She could hear their footsteps tapping gently on the tile floor. They had come to a conclusion so quickly that it took her breath away. And it also made her wonder if Elizabeth's accident was truly an accident. She pulled out her laptop and turned it on. While it booted up, she sipped her coffee and started in on her muffin. As soon as her computer was up, she opened her emails, hoping to see something from Mary. But there was nothing.

She frowned. "Now what do I do?" Was Mary avoiding her? Or was she just so exhausted that she couldn't deal with anything more? Or was she worried Faith would ask more of her than she could give?

What Faith needed was the name of Laszlo's detective friend because she'd really like to see Elizabeth's accident report. She pulled out her phone and texted Cade. **If you're getting accident reports on Laszlo's father, can you get one for me on Elizabeth?**

And then she quickly sent a second text. **Please. I've asked Elizabeth's sister already, but she's not responding. I heard you in the hall talking about the SUV that was potentially the weapon used to run down Laszlo's father. It amazes me how quickly you got rid of all the excess information and got to the core of things. And that's what I have to know. Was Elizabeth in an accident**

or was it intentional? I don't know who else to ask.

Instead of getting an answer, her phone rang. It was Cade. "Thank you for calling me back," she said quietly. "I know this is a big request …"

"What's her last name?"

"Elizabeth Brown."

"That's not a Norwegian name."

"Her mother remarried and came over here."

"We're almost at the police station now. I can ask the detective to contact you. I doubt he'd give that information to me."

"Oh, I never thought of that," she said.

"It's not that big a deal. We'll see if we can get it from him. The best would be that he sends it to you though."

"Is there any reason I couldn't have a copy?" she asked worriedly. "I wouldn't want to get him in trouble."

"I don't think there are any laws against it. But I'll see what he says."

"Let me give you my email." She quickly ran it off for him.

"You want to text that to me instead?" he asked, when she went quiet. "Then I'll have it to give to him."

She rang off, then quickly sent him a text. And sent another one saying thanks. She was still working on her piece of fruit and cup of coffee when the email came in from the detective. Sure enough, attached was the accident report. Delighted, she put down her coffee to open the attachment. And winced. Apparently Elizabeth was going too fast and missed a corner. She'd spun out, flipped around and ended up in a ditch.

"Well, at least it was her own fault, not somebody else hitting her on purpose." Although that was small comfort.

But it did make Faith feel better that somebody hadn't pushed her off the road and neither had Elizabeth hurt anybody else.

Faith quickly replied to the detective, thanking him for sending the report.

A few minutes later she got a text from Cade. **Did he send it?**

Yes, he did. Elizabeth was involved in a single-vehicle accident. She spun out on a corner, taking it too fast, and hit a ditch. Nobody else was injured. Nobody else was involved.

Good. That should make you feel better.

It does. Now if she'd wake up and be just fine, then my life would be about perfect.

He didn't answer after that. And why should he? There wasn't anything to say.

CADE SAT IN the police station, a copy of the report on Henry in his hand. The trouble was, it was in Norwegian. Although English appeared to be spoken everywhere, he wasn't surprised to see a report like this in English. He picked up his phone and sent Faith a message. **Was your report in Norwegian?**

It was in English.

Oh, good.

Cade put away his phone and turned to look at the detective. So far, he'd shown no signs he spoke English. But he had a good enough grasp of it to write the simple details of Elizabeth's report on the same PDF in English for Faith's use. "Thank you for sending Faith a copy of the Elizabeth Brown accident report," he said smoothly in English. "And

Faith really appreciated getting it in English."

He felt Talon startle with surprise beside him. The detective tossed him a glance and nodded but kept talking to Laszlo.

Cade held up their current accident report. "I have to admit to being impressed at how much English is spoken here."

Talon opened up the laptop he always carried in his backpack and sat down to boot it up. They took a look at the report only to realize this was an even simpler accident report than Elizabeth's. And maybe nobody did very much in the way of forensic assessment on accidents over here. According to the report, Henry had been walking at night with his dogs. He was struck from behind, the blow sending him into the ditch, where several rocks connected with his face.

The English wasn't perfect, but it was all they needed. "No sign of a vehicle afterward, no witnesses."

Talon nodded. "It's exactly as we thought." He powered down his laptop and put it away.

Cade studied the accident report in his hands, wondering at its simplicity. But then he guessed there were many just like this one at home too. He folded the paperwork and tucked it in his pocket.

It didn't seem like Laszlo and the detective were done talking, but they shook hands; then Laszlo stood. He started to walk out of the station and turned to look at the two of them. "Are you ready?"

Cade snorted. "We were ready a long time ago."

Laszlo had the grace to look ashamed. "Sorry, it's so much easier to discuss these things in Norwegian when I'm here."

"I speak several languages," Talon said. "But Norwegian

isn't one of them."

"English is spoken everywhere but Norwegian is easier for him. But the detective will run the numbers for us and see if he can get us access to the city cameras."

"When will we know?"

"He'll call me or Jair. He has a meeting with the superintendent this afternoon. He'll ask then."

They stepped out onto the street to find it was getting dark.

"Food?" Talon asked. "Are we staying in town until we hear from him in regard to the close-circuit cameras, or will we go to your family's home?"

Laszlo stood with his arms crossed for a long moment. "If he can get us access soon, I'd rather stay and go through that."

"How did your family do all day?"

Laszlo shot him a look. "I had two of the neighbors bring over food for them. They'll send me the bills." Once again, Laszlo picked out a place for them to have dinner and ordered for himself and his two friends. And, as before, it was plenty of food and tasted great.

Dinner done, they relaxed a bit, talking in hushed tones about Henry's case, when Laszlo's phone rang. He pulled it out, looked at the number and answered. "Jair, what's up?" A moment later he turned toward Cade and Talon with a big grin. "We can see the camera feeds." He stood, leaving money for the food and the tip, and headed outside. Cade and Talon followed.

CHAPTER 5

FAITH HEARD THE hospital room door open. It nudged her out of her dozing state. Six hours sleep, even in a real bed, still wasn't enough. She glanced up to see a nurse once again entering the private room. Faith leaned toward her and said, "Still no change. But she's also not worse. Surely that's a good sign."

The nurse smiled encouragingly. "It is." She took Elizabeth's vitals then turned to look at Faith. "She is doing quite a bit better. Maybe she's aware of your presence, and it is helping her heal."

Faith beamed, even though she knew it was just kind words. "She's a beautiful person," she said. "I'm so sorry this happened to her."

"The doctor will be in soon." The nurse checked her watch. "He's running late, but I hope to see him by dinnertime."

Faith nodded. "Maybe we'll know more by then."

The nurse nodded and quietly withdrew. Sitting here beside her friend, Faith had lots of time to consider the shortness of life. Planning to live to old age didn't cut it. Elizabeth was proof of that. And just because she was holding on didn't mean she would make a full recovery. Any recovery would be lovely though. But so often there were injuries that took years to recover from. She understood

Elizabeth couldn't pull out of this coma because of the drugs, but Faith would like to believe that Elizabeth was calmer with Faith at her side. But again, it was just likely positive thinking. When the door opened yet again, she assumed it was the nurse.

She looked up to see Mary walking back in with quite an odd look on her face. "What's the matter, Mary?"

Mary gave a headshake. "I just can't believe she's still alive," she said softly. She walked over to her sister and gently stroked her fingers. "My mother and I came and said goodbye because the doctor said there was no hope."

"There's always hope," Faith said.

Mary shrugged. "Of course we know that. But that doesn't mean in every case it'll happen. It feels like we're just delaying the inevitable."

That was hardly fair. Faith enjoyed just being at Elizabeth's side, and Mary hadn't been in all day. But then maybe Faith was judging her too harshly. Elizabeth had been close to her sister but not as close as Elizabeth was to Faith. Then that was often the way of it.

"I wanted to thank you for letting me know," Faith said quietly. "I'm so glad I'm here for her."

In her mind she refused to say the word "die," but it seemed like Mary wanted Faith to acknowledge that her sister wouldn't make it. Trouble was, Faith was stubborn. She was pragmatic, but she sure wouldn't give up without a good fight. "Having said that," she said firmly, "I believe Elizabeth will pull out of this."

Mary glanced at her with pity in her eyes. "You know that's not likely, right?"

Faith smiled, infusing positivity into her voice "Whether it's likely or not, I firmly believe it will happen. I also believe she can hear us." She smiled down at Elizabeth. "She's too full of life and joy. She has too much in her to have her beautiful life cut so short."

"Accidents happen," Mary said dismissively. "I know that all too well."

That's when Faith remembered how Mary's husband had died in a freak accident when walking along a street. Scaffolding had fallen down on top of him. Impulsively Faith stood and placed a caring hand on Mary's shoulder. "Yes, accidents do happen. But they don't happen to everyone all the time. We must let Elizabeth have her chance to fight."

But Mary seemed destined to believe the worst. "I just don't want you so devastated after you build up all this hope." She motioned to the machines. "Without the drugs and the machines, she wouldn't be here now."

"But she is here now," Faith said, keeping her voice calm, when all she wanted to do was yell at Mary, tell her to smarten up and to be positive. But negative people were more common than positive people. And their sour attitudes permeated every sector of life. Faith didn't know why she should be surprised. She'd heard Elizabeth talk about Mary's pessimism often. Faith just hadn't realized how it would impact something like Elizabeth's accident. And Faith had to wonder, what if something happened to Faith? Would anybody care? Would anybody sit at her side and try to keep her around?

Her own mother was as negative as Mary and Faith's mother and would likely tell the doctors to let Faith go. Why put anybody through all that darn suffering only to die anyway? Just as her mother had prophesies of everything in the world crashing down on Faith for having dared to become a pilot. It was a sad attitude. And Faith knew that many people would look at her hopeful attitude and say she was not grounded in reality.

She'd always been an optimist. Always had been somebody who believed in something better down the road. And she couldn't give up hope on her best friend. Because, from what she could see, Faith was the only help her friend had.

Mary turned and walked back to the door. "You have my email address," she said. "You can let me know if there's any change in her condition." And she walked out.

Faith would have thought Mary was nothing but cold and callous except she heard the sniffles as she left. Maybe along with being a negative personality, Mary couldn't handle disasters or grief. Maybe she cared *too* much. It was easy to be judgmental when other people reacted differently than you did. At the same time, it made Faith feel very sad for Elizabeth to have such negative people in her life—in her immediate family even.

Faith walked over to her friend's bedside and gently stroked Elizabeth's cheek. "So much easier to bury yourself in the kids you loved than to be with a family, so depressed all the time and so focused on the negative, wasn't it?"

She cast her mind back to when she'd first met Elizabeth. The two girls had been sitting at basketball tryouts. Both had wanted to be on the team, but neither had planned to attempt it because they came from a world where it was normal *not* to try, since the foregone conclusion was that you would never make it anyway. But somehow they ended up challenging each other to try out anyway.

The funny thing was, neither made it onto the team. They were awful at basketball. But because they made an attempt, they didn't feel bad. The whole point of picking a basketball team was to pick the best players. Or at least those with potential. Who would have guessed that what came out of that meeting was that both girls had found each other? And realized that so much of their upbringing had conditioned the way they were looking at life.

And they made a pact back then to not get sucked into their respective family's negativity, to do things because they wanted to and not to avoid them because others had told them they couldn't.

Faith sat down beside Elizabeth. "Remember that boy you really liked?" she asked with a big smile. "Remember how terrified you were that he wouldn't like you? And you desperately wanted to go to the dance with him. Every time he came close to you, you ran. Until I dared you to invite him yourself. Dared you not to be such a scaredy-cat, to go after something you really wanted." Faith chuckled at the memory.

"And he said yes, didn't he? You were the happiest, proudest girl ever. And even then your mom laughed at you, telling you that you shouldn't have asked him because it wasn't feminine and it showed he didn't really like you enough to ask you out himself. You were so depressed when she said that. And I understood because it's exactly what my mother would have said too. But just as I challenged you to go and to have a good time and challenged you to go into teaching because you love children—even though your mother said, 'Why bother when you can't have any of your own? Why put yourself through that torment?'—it was you who pushed me to go into flight school. And I'm so glad you did. And I'm so glad I went. But I'm most glad I found you. And I'm so glad to be here with you right now."

As she sat here, gently stroking Elizabeth's fingers,

caught down memory lane, she could feel the fingers wiggle underneath hers. She slid her fingers between Elizabeth's. "Elizabeth, are you in there?"

The fingers wiggled again.

Faith gasped. "Was that just a reflex? Are you responding to my voice, to my question? If you are, squeeze my fingers."

And the fingers just lay there. Lifeless. And yet there was such a sense of peace on Elizabeth's face.

Faith didn't know if that was a case of having made a great effort and achieved something, like wiggling her fingers, or if it was a goodbye, and she was ready to walk off this Earth.

For a long moment, Faith sat, urging Elizabeth to try again. But there was no more movement. Faith didn't know if she should mention it to the nurse or doctor when she saw them next, already knowing they'd tell her it was just nerves and not a conscious reaction.

But it made Faith more determined than ever to stay at Elizabeth's side. Because who knew? Maybe there was one more miracle to be had in this hospital room. And maybe Faith had just enough hope for both of them.

THE MEN WERE seated in the officer's control room, the screens in front of them. They were tracking down the license plates on the two rented SUVs as a starting point. The detective said they could sit behind the officer as he searched the traffic cameras for the vehicle they were looking for. The theory being that the more eyes, the better, but they weren't to interfere in the investigation in any way.

Cade and Talon had agreed, as had Laszlo. But Laszlo's

chair was slightly more forward as he sat closer to the control room officer, the two of them speaking the same language. The screens, a dozen in all, flashed as the computer searched out the license plates. The monitor on the left started to flash more so, as it picked up the license plate of the first SUV leaving the airport. It tracked and then lost the vehicle. The one in the middle picked up the same license plate heading through the main intersection from the airport, out on the highway toward downtown Oslo.

After that was only darkness for a long time. But when it came to an intersection with a roundabout heading north and south, the SUV was picked up going in the direction of the small town where Henry lived.

Laszlo tapped the monitor. "He's still going in the right direction."

The monitors had picked up the other SUV license plate through the city cameras, but it appeared to be stopping frequently just within the city itself. The officer made a couple comments on the locations.

Laszlo nodded. "It looks like the second SUV rental is sticking to some of the less-popular areas."

"Drugs?"

"Hard to say. He is alone."

The SUV was parked outside the warehouse district for four hours. It was picked up again going through different intersections. And very quickly it returned to the airport. At that point they had no way to know if he changed vehicles, went to a hotel, stayed there until his flight out or took an earlier flight or was traveling under a different name.

There were so many unknowns, they were just guessing. Until Laszlo picked up the first SUV on the next day, heading back out to his town. "This is his second trip. In two days."

"This trip is in the morning."

They took several screen shots of the license plate, the front and the side of the SUV, and when they caught it on the cameras returning to the city, Laszlo yelled, "Freeze." The officer froze the image and then had to back it up frame-by-frame. There was a decent photo of the front right-hand side of the SUV. And there was a slight dent on the front corner. Everybody sat back and stared at that for a long moment.

"Son of a bitch," Cade snapped. "That's where he hit your father, isn't it?"

"Most likely but we'll check with the rental agency." After a short lull, Laszlo stood with a start, his fists clenched to match his jaw. "That SOB took a goddamn tank of an SUV to run over my father, with twice the body mass of most cars on the road. To run over a seventy-four-year-old man walking alongside the road." Talon shook his head, adding, "It's a miracle he survived."

No one spoke. What could be said?

After that Talon took to silently pacing the small control room.

Now that they had confirmed which SUV had been the weapon used in Henry's attack, they focused on every image they had picked up, including until it was returned to the airport. What they were looking for was an image of the driver's face. As he came through the cameras leaving for the airport parking lot, he ducked his head a bit, and they caught part of his lower jaw. He had a beard and a moustache, hair that curled to his shoulders. But they couldn't get a picture of his eyes. It was in the smoked windshield section. With that printed, along with the other photographs, the men stood, thanked the officer and walked out.

"What do you think?" Cade asked.

"I think it's our best bet," Laszlo said. "Now let's confirm people who may have seen him. See if we can get more of his face somehow."

"Any chance of running that through facial recognition?"

"The officer said, because it's only a partial and because the beard obscures a lot of the important facial markers, it probably won't work. In cases like that, they need the forehead, brows and nose markers. But he will run it through and see."

The men nodded.

"I don't think it's an accident that we don't have a full facial image. However, we should show this to the hotel staff. They should have cameras as well."

Laszlo nodded. "I'll see if I can get the detective to do that." He reached for his phone as they walked outside to find it dark. Laszlo spoke to the detective for several long moments. Then he turned back to Cade and Talon. "I think we should head back."

"You feeling nervous about your father?"

"Not yet," he said. "But the fact that this asshole left him alive, to me that means either he was careless, thinking the old man couldn't possibly survive, or he was on a schedule and couldn't afford any more time."

"If it was deliberate, wouldn't he have stopped the vehicle and made sure your father was dead?"

"Honestly most people would have thought he was already. His pulse was so faint that the ambulance paramedics had trouble picking it up. Even they thought he was probably gone."

Cade and Talon nodded. "Fairly common in an older person."

"There's old, and then there's old. My dad has always had low blood pressure issues." Laszlo's phone rang. He answered it. "Jair, what's up?" He spoke for a few moments and then hung up. "My father's gone to bed. His day was okay. There is leftover food if we want to eat at home."

The two shook their heads. "No, because that's a meal for them tomorrow," Cade said. "We had an early dinner. Honestly I'm okay with just a sandwich later on."

"In that case, I can make that at home, but we do need groceries soon."

They got in the vehicle and headed toward Henry's house.

"I suggest we stop at any gas stations or points of interest along the way to see if somebody may have seen this guy. We're driving in at the same time of day the attacker would have been driving as well."

Laszlo nodded. "Good point."

Up ahead was a gas station. He pulled off to the side, picked up the pictures and exited. Cade and Talon were right behind him. Cade worried about Laszlo. It was one thing to track down answers. But it was another thing entirely when the answers were difficult. Cade was still reeling from the thoughts that somebody had attacked all their families.

As soon as they got back to Laszlo's place, Cade wanted to make some calls and see if anybody had an update. The time change was brutal. But, in this case, it worked to their benefit.

Laszlo was ahead of them, just enough that he was already talking with a man by the time Cade entered the building. The clerk looked at the photos and shrugged.

"He doesn't remember," Laszlo said. "He said there are not many people at night unless it's tourists."

"Well, it was a rental vehicle," Cade said.

Laszlo reminded him of that. But the young man shook his head. "Okay, no help there."

They hopped in the vehicle and went on to the next gas station just on the outskirts of town. They pulled in to ask the same questions. But this time they got a completely different response. The store and gas station were run by an older man and his sons.

One of the sons nodded. "That was about a month ago."

"Why would you remember that?" Laszlo asked.

"Because he was really arrogant. There was just something about him." The younger man shrugged. "At the time I thought he was a snobby American. The kind who would flip you off. He had such a dismissive attitude to everything we had in the store. As if he expected a full line of French cuisine here for him or something."

The men nodded. "Do you remember his face at all?"

He tapped the photo. "That face. But he had a hat on. There was something about his eyes. I can't remember the color, but it was that look."

"Look?" Cade asked.

Laszlo continued to translate.

"Yes. Cold, dead almost."

The father reached over and patted him on his hand.

Laszlo turned to Cade. "His father says he has a great imagination."

"Cameras?"

Laszlo asked then turned to the men. "They only keep for 30 days. And we're past that now."

The men thanked the three attendants and turned back to the vehicle.

"Thoughts?" Talon asked as they all got inside the car, sitting there for a moment.

"Well, it was him. We just don't have any proof."

"No, but if the detective can track him down from when he first left the rental agency, the license plate will confirm the damage wasn't there prior to the rental. The agency should have a driver's license with a photo ID for us."

"How long will it take him to get that information?"

"Unfortunately the detective has a life. And he's off duty. He went home to have dinner with his wife and kids. I really don't know if he'll do anything about this tonight. I don't know if anybody at the rental agency will be there at this hour. It'll have to wait until morning."

Cade groaned. "You know? It would be much easier if the world worked on a twenty-four-hour clock."

Talon smiled. "It would. Unless you were called in to work outside of the schedule we wanted to work."

They were still wrangling when they pulled up to Laszlo's home. They walked inside to see Jair sitting, waiting for them. Cade hated to see the young man so pale and nervous. His face lit up with relief when he saw Laszlo.

Immediately a flurry of Norwegian flew from his mouth. Laszlo talked in a calming voice. By way of explanation he said, "He spoke with his friend, the detective. Jair is worried we'll be in danger."

Cade could understand that. Laszlo and Jair had already been through enough and had come close to losing their father. "I don't think we're in danger. But has he considered that maybe he and your father are?"

The brothers spoke a little longer, as Talon and Cade

headed toward the kitchen.

"Has anybody considered that maybe the accident was enough?" Talon asked Cade.

"Laszlo *is* suffering." Cade nodded.

"His brother already had a terminal disease," Talon stated. "His father is now injured and probably will suffer a lot over the next years that he has left. And that, in turn, just twisted the screws tighter into Laszlo."

"Meaning that he will be tortured more by the hired gunman leaving his father alive, now in this broken state?" Cade asked, confirming.

"Exactly. Maybe the hired gun didn't mean to kill him," Talon said. "Maybe, even if he had killed him, that would be fine too, but maybe he's thinking this is even better."

Cade shook his head. "That's cold."

Talon looked at him. "But it's the truth."

CHAPTER 6

I T WAS LATE when Faith stumbled out of the hospital towards the hotel. She'd stayed with Elizabeth as long as she could today. The doctors had come to do their evening rounds, but they saw no change in Elizabeth and expressed how she wasn't likely to change again. Still, Faith had stayed for another hour, just talking with Elizabeth, and then felt the fatigue pull. Not to mention the fact Faith hadn't eaten in hours.

She gathered up her stuff and headed outside, smiling at the brace of fresh air. She walked across to the hotel and stepped into the small coffee shop. She wasn't terribly hungry but knew she needed to eat something. A bowl of soup and salad would suffice nicely.

Upstairs in her room, she pulled out her laptop and sat on the bed. With her cell phone beside her, she caught up on some backlogged stuff. She filled her mom and a couple friends in who were concerned about her and Elizabeth.

Thinking of friends, knowing Cade didn't quite fit that bill—though he had been concerned enough to get her the accident report and to get her set up in this hotel—she sent him a text, asking if he was okay and if he'd learned anything about Laszlo's father's accident. She was surprised when he responded quickly.

Maybe. We're running through the details now.

There's a chance I found a vehicle, but it was a rental.

A rental? So you should be able to track it then? Right? She hit the Send button, thinking at least he was getting some answers.

Responding, he called her. Surprised and yet delighted, she said, "You didn't have to call me. I know you're busy."

"Did you check the time? It's past eleven here." There was a note of humor in his voice. "I wouldn't have called you, but obviously you're still awake."

"The time change is quite brutal, isn't it?"

"It can be," he agreed. "And we did find out some stuff today, but we're not likely to get any good answers."

"At least Laszlo has a chance to see his father, and hopefully his father will be okay."

"He is at home and healing. But he's older. He's definitely a senior, and this is very difficult for him. He has the home care attendants who come in and help him too."

She winced. "I don't know what's worse, accidents with old people where they'll struggle to recover—and maybe not ever quite fully—or something like Elizabeth, where she was young and vibrant, with a whole life ahead of her."

"Neither are good. They just are. And that makes them bad news for all of us. When the people we care about are hurting, it's never good." His voice lowered. "And, of course, it's still supposition. Just because we pinpointed a rental vehicle that went out to the accident site doesn't mean we have any way to prove that its driver was the person who did it."

"And a rental vehicle, does that give you a picture?"

"Not necessarily. But maybe."

She frowned at that. "Meaning, a driver's license should have been used to rent the vehicle. I can see that."

"It doesn't mean it does us any good. It was a month ago. The person flew out again most likely. And he could have rented the vehicle using false papers. It's a simple process for anyone who knows what they are doing."

"That's even worse. Playing the tourist is easy, as they come and go and are never seen again."

"True enough. When are you heading home?" he asked rather abruptly.

"Well, I have the week off. I'm just not too sure how long Elizabeth will be in this state."

"That sucks. Just because she's like this now doesn't mean there won't be changes over the next few weeks."

"Exactly. She could be like this for quite a while."

"Well, for your sake and Elizabeth's, I hope she recovers while you are here to be with her."

"Wouldn't that be wonderful?" she said.

"Yes, it would. For now, I'll say good night," Cade said quietly. "Hope tomorrow is a better day for you."

She chuckled. "You too." She hung up.

But she couldn't sleep now. She thought about all the elements that went into a hit-and-run and the things the police had to find in order to track down the driver. It was tough. On impulse she typed a message, **I know it's a long shot, but could you send me his photo? I just want to make sure I don't know who he is either.**

We're waiting for a full-face photo came Cade's reply. **But attached is the one we found from the traffic cameras.**

She transferred it to her laptop and brought it up. She stared at it for a long moment. It was almost familiar. There was just that eerie tickling awareness going down her spine that said maybe she did know this person. But she had to think about why. And just how sure of it was she?

He texted again. **Any luck?**

Slowly, not sure she should, she replied. **Maybe. ... Thinking about it ...**

Instantly the phone rang in her hand. "You've seen him? You recognize him?"

"I'm not sure," she said. "Maybe ..."

"Maybe?" he asked in ominous tones. "What do you mean by that?"

"His face, what there is of it, is familiar. That's all I can say. Something about the way I can only see the lower jaw."

"When could you possibly have seen him?"

She chuckled. "I'm a pilot. I see people all the time. Sure, I spend a lot of my time in the front of the plane, but I always stand at the door to greet my passengers and to take time to look at them. I also see them when I come through the waiting lines. I also work with a ton of people."

His voice was thoughtful. "Do you think you've flown him before?"

"I'm not sure. Let me sleep on it. I'll see what pops in my head during the night." With that she hung up again.

The face bothered her. She couldn't think why. But instinctively she knew the eyes above had a cold, almost dead look to them. Like he didn't give a shit about anything. She'd seen those eyes, that look. Now, if only she could remember when and where.

The trouble was, frustration didn't help her sleep. An hour later she was still awake. Finally she fell asleep, but it was to nightmares of strange faces and bearded men weaving in and out of her consciousness, and just as she was starting to wake up, they would get hit by a vehicle.

Finally it was morning, though only six. She sat up to

read her texts. There was no going back to sleep for her. The little bit she'd had made her more tired. And unfortunately she had no answer for Cade as to who the man in the photo was.

She got up and had a quick shower. Then she brought up her laptop to check the news around the world and to check her emails. It appeared everything was calm. She often wondered about that phenomenon. Her world was in complete chaos, and yet the rest of the world just coasted on its axis, as if nobody out there gave a damn that she was on rocky ground. It was probably the way it was supposed to be. You had to deal with your own personal chaos in your own way.

She dressed quickly, pocketed her phone, repacked her laptop and headed downstairs.

The receptionist called her as she was about to walk out. "You didn't say how many nights you were staying," the man said in a guttural English.

She smiled. "I don't really know. At least tonight though."

He nodded and plastered a big smile on his face. "Nice to have you."

It was seven-thirty when she walked out of the hotel. She crossed the street and walked the block to the hospital. Nobody had contacted her through the night, but that didn't mean Elizabeth had gone through her night easily.

As she walked to Elizabeth's room, one of the nurses smiled at her. "She had a good night."

Relieved, Faith smiled. "That is such good news. Surely she'll pull through this."

The nurse shrugged. "The doctors are hopeful. But it's far too soon to tell. It's easy for us to see this as a positive sign, but it can turn just as quickly the other way."

The nurse walked past, and Faith slipped into Elizabeth's room. There was just something about the smell of a hospital. However, the attendant noises were reassuring, hearing the machines and the various sounds they made as they beeped and droned beside Elizabeth. Faith walked to the foot of her friend's bed and studied her face.

"It's me again, Elizabeth. Faith. I'm back to visit for a while."

There was no recognition on her friend's face, no stirring of the fingers, nothing. But she did look more rested. As if she was content to let the drugs keep her under and was no longer fighting to surface or was no longer in pain, the lines of worry and stress had eased back from her face. When Faith had first arrived, Elizabeth had had an almost contorted tightness to her cheeks. Whereas, right now, she had a relaxed look to her face.

As Faith sat, wishing she'd swung by the cafeteria to pick up coffee and something to eat, the nurse popped her head in and said, "We'll be bringing breakfast around for the patients soon. Can I get you a tray?"

Surprised and touched, Faith answered, "Thank you. I would appreciate that."

And the nurse disappeared just as fast.

While she waited, Faith brought up her laptop and once again took a look at the picture Cade had sent her. This time the sense of recognition was even stronger. But the answer to where she knew him from and who he was stayed just out of her reach. She set the laptop on the small table beside her as her phone rang. It was Cade.

"No, I don't know who, where or why, but, yes, I do recognize him," she said calmly. "And I know that's absolutely no help. All I can tell you is that it's bugging me, but I haven't come up with any answers."

"If you do, let me know," he said. "And, by the way, how is your friend?"

"The nurses were a little more hopeful this morning. Every day Elizabeth manages to stay alive and to fight is a day her body manages to heal that much more."

"I'll call you later then," Cade said. "But don't forget this is really important. If there's any way to dislodge that information from your brain …"

"I'll try," she said firmly. "But, like I said, I've seen a lot of people."

"Think about that look. And where else you might have seen it. Somebody's driver? A passenger with the hat down low? Somebody who was arguing? Somebody at a ticket counter giving people trouble?"

"You think he's an argumentative type?" she asked quietly. "I know the eyes are about all that are missing in this picture, and yet I know they are dead. Cold, like they don't give a shit about anything or anyone. What I don't remember is how and where I have that impression."

"Interesting," he said slowly. "Another potential witness said the same thing."

"I'll dredge my memory some more. But I don't know any way to unlock that little bit of information. You and I both know what it's like to have something sit just outside your reach, where you can't quite put your finger on it, but it's there nonetheless."

"All I ask is that you keep trying," he said firmly. And with that he hung up.

She stared down at the picture and froze. Instantly memories came flooding back. Cade had been right. She'd seen him when driving. Back home. In Santa Fe, New Mexico. This man had been driving a car. And she'd almost hit him accidentally because he cut into her lane. He'd followed her down the block. When she'd parked at the bank, he'd pulled in behind her. She'd been unnerved, wondering exactly what he might do. She hadn't hit him, but it had been a close encounter.

At the same time, he'd also been at fault for cutting into her space. It had shocked both of them. But there was something about the look on his face. She had wondered if she should talk to him. Then he hopped out of the vehicle, pulled his hat down low and called out, "Learn to drive better, bitch."

She'd stiffened at the time, shot him a look, realized his shoulders were set with anger, but it was those eyes, that glimpse she'd caught. He tilted his hat back as she opened her mouth to apologize, and, when she saw that look, it said she better not say the wrong thing. She stared at him for at least ten seconds, then she turned and walked into the bank.

Inside the bank she'd looked out the window to see if he was still there. He was, but then he drove away.

She didn't have anything to go by other than that chance encounter. But there had been something about him that had left an indelible mark. She picked up her phone and called Cade back. "I remember where I saw him." She quickly explained.

"In Santa Fe?"

"Yes. I was heading to the bank."

"Any idea when?"

She sighed. "The day after I came back and shared the cab with you."

"Just a few days ago?" he asked, almost in a roar.

"Yes. Why?"

"Well, if it's the same person we think is doing this, it could mean another friend of ours is in danger." He ended the call abruptly.

She stared at the photo on her laptop, then at the dead phone in her hand and realized the man she'd seen outside the bank could be capable of doing anything. And she was delighted he was a hell of a long way from her right now.

CADE TURNED TO face the others. They all sat around the kitchen table, data sheets spread all across its surface. Laszlo said, "She saw him?"

Cade nodded. "In short, she said she would never forget the dead, cold look in his eyes." He quickly shared the little bit she'd remembered, then added, "I never thought to ask any more questions. I was just shocked she recognized him."

"Coincidence?"

"Not necessarily. Not if he's coming after us individually, after our families."

"But we're not all in Santa Fe."

"No, but that doesn't mean he isn't keeping tabs on those of us who are."

"Badger?" they all said in unison.

"He's the most vulnerable right now."

Cade was nodding, already had his phone in hand, dialing Erick. "I know it's late, but I have to forewarn him."

A sleepy voice answered.

"Erick, there's been a strange development."

Cade told him about the face they'd found on camera. "I sent it to you, but I don't know if you've had a chance to look at it yet. However, Faith says she remembers seeing him in New Mexico."

"What?" Erick mumbled, as if shaking the sleep out of his brain. "Who is Faith?"

Cade shrugged, not sure how to explain. And that's when Laszlo spoke across the table in a louder voice. "Cade's girlfriend. The pilot he shared the cab with the other day."

"What the hell is she doing over there with you? Did I miss something here?" There was outrage in his tone, as if somebody had slipped one past him.

Cade smiled. "No, her best friend was in a bad accident. She came over, hoping to see her before she passed away. Instead her friend is clinging to life, and Faith is clinging to the hospital bed beside her."

"And you just thought, out of the blue, it was a good idea to show her the photo of a man who ran down Laszlo's father?" Erick sounded as if he wondered about Cade's mental health.

Cade sighed. "I know it sounds stupid. But we helped her a couple times, and then somehow we ended up in the discussion of getting accident reports, and she asked for the report from her best friend's accident. We got that for her, and then she heard us discussing chopping down the number of rental units to investigate to just a couple. Anyway, I ended up showing her the picture from the city cameras. It's only his lower face. I figured that, since she was a pilot, she might have seen him in the airport. And she recognized him."

"And she's sure it's him?"

"Yes, she said she recognized him."

"Then I need to see that photo, and we should find out exactly what bank and any other details she can give us about the car he was driving, how old he is, etc. So that's your job as soon as you can." Erick added, "I was trying to sleep, but apparently that's not happening." His tone was all business now. "Are we assuming somebody else here is in trouble?"

"We must assume he might be going after somebody else, one of us. I'm not sure who's got family in Santa Fe right now, but what we don't want is for him to go after girlfriends. None of us have wives, but two of you now have somebody you care about."

"And, if he's involved—like we're thinking from our original accident—he'll know about Kat and Honey."

"Exactly," Cade said. "Both those women need to be aware and hypervigilant." He waited a moment and asked, "What about Badger? How's he doing?"

"He's doing better. The blood clot was a game-changer. But now he has to face surgery again."

There was silence at the table. Laszlo, Talon and Cade all exchanged glances. "Shit. If you get a chance, tell him we are there with him. And make sure you tell Kat to be on the lookout. For her and for Badger. She's already been through hell. We can't have somebody going after her too."

"I'll handle our people in Santa Fe. You guys find out everything you can about Laszlo's father. Sounds like it was worth going there after all. But it might be time to leave, to see if we can track this asshole back here."

"Sure."

"Oh, and, Cade, just in case, make sure nobody gets the impression you and Faith are an item."

"She's over here, so I highly doubt it. That guy is back with you. I'd be more worried about Honey and Kat and Badger."

"I'll also do a search on all of us, to make sure there's no more family here."

"Okay. I'll get on the phone again with Faith and gather more details." Cade put down his phone. "It makes a sick kind of sense that this asshole would have gone back to Badger's hometown if he's trying to make maximum pain."

"So he kills family members, and now you're thinking he may go after girlfriends?"

Laszlo whistled. "How sick is this guy? I mean, if he already blew us all up two years ago, why does he still care so much now about hurting us further? We've all suffered more than any of us ever deserved to suffer."

"Because he's still hating," Cade said, slowly working his way through it. "For whatever reason he still hates us. And to know we're still alive, still doing okay, while he's not, ... it's eating at him."

"Nobody hates us like this."

"Somebody does," Cade said. "And the sooner we find out who, the better."

Talon said slowly, "Erick'll handle Santa Fe, right?"

Cade nodded. "He's also doing a search on all our families, ensuring nobody else is in New Mexico. I don't know how much family any of us have left. I know Geir transplanted to Santa Fe."

"He moved to just outside, but that won't make a damn bit of difference. Somebody needs to warn him."

"And Jager is still on a blackout, I imagine. At least Erick didn't say otherwise."

"We need to ask him. And we have to get to the bottom of this fast. Before somebody else ends up dead."

CHAPTER 7

FAITH SAT BESIDE Elizabeth all morning. Not once did Mary show up. Not once did Elizabeth's mother show up. Were they both so sure Elizabeth would pass away that they couldn't be bothered to come and spend what time she had left here? It really bothered Faith. At the same time, she knew she had no right to judge. It was just so damn hard not to.

There'd been no other communication from Cade. But she hadn't been able to stop thinking about the man outside the Santa Fe bank. She'd been extremely unnerved at the time. But she hadn't seen him since. She remembered something about his car but not a whole lot.

Her phone rang. Cade.

"Can you give me any more details about the man you saw? The vehicle?"

"I was just thinking about that. It was a small black Lexus."

"Do you happen to know anything about car models?"

She laughed. "No, I don't. I'd probably recognize it if I were to search them online. And there was a *G* and a *T* in the license plate number."

"Anything else?"

"He was tall. I remember that. Lanky build."

"How tall?"

"I'd say over six foot. Kind of scrawny when I say lanky build. You know? The tall, thin guy. But he looked strong. More like a wire restrained. Somebody you wouldn't want to underestimate."

"Hair color?"

She frowned. "The beard was a brown with a slight reddish tinge. He was definitely a Caucasian male, but I don't know a whole lot more." She sounded apologetic. "The Lexus had a soft top," she added suddenly.

"What made you remember that?"

"Because I was thinking, when we almost hit each other, that it would damage the roof and then realized it was a soft-top convertible."

"What kind of hat?"

That stopped her. She frowned, thinking back. "I don't know. Just like a baseball style. But I don't remember seeing any kind of a name or ad printed on it."

"Clothing?"

"Jeans." She thought back to when she had watched from the bank window. She'd taken a close look at him. "He had scars on the back of his right hand."

"How did you see that?" he asked.

"When I was staring at him from inside the bank, he was thrumming his fingers on the roof of his Lexus. He was standing behind the open door, glaring at me. But I remember his fingers were long, muscled. And they were red, maybe dark lines up and down his hands, as if he'd been recently badly scratched."

"So maybe not scars as much as newer injuries?"

"Yeah."

"So then how do you know he had jeans on?" He sounded apologetic. "I'm not doubting what you saw. I just need to know that what you saw was real."

"Because of the Lexus and that he was tall. I saw the belt buckle over the jeans."

"Belt buckle?"

"Yeah, it was weird. It was large, almost like a symbol of some kind. Like wings but not. I don't know. I just saw it in one very fast glance, so you can't really count on anything I'm saying here."

"Shirt?"

"Button-up, rolled up at the sleeves. I could see most of the forearm. Hairy."

"Color?"

"Blue-and-white check." She surprised herself with all the details. But now that he'd mentioned the shirt, she could see the man quite clearly. "He had some kind of a necklace on."

"And you saw that how?"

"Top couple buttons of the shirt were open. There was a white undershirt beneath, and it was a metal chain. There was some metal hanging off the chain, maybe two pieces at the end of the chain."

There was silence on the other end. Then Cade said softly, "Two metal pieces? Like dog tags?"

"Yes, that's it. That means he was ex-military of some kind, wasn't he?"

"It could be."

"But it might not be, right? I don't know if this guy is one of those poser kind of guys who just likes to look tough. But I can tell you that the attitude, the set of his shoulders, the firmness to his jaw and the twitching muscle on the side of his face meant he was pissed."

"But you didn't hit the Lexus?"

"No. I swear I didn't."

Cade was silent for a few moments.

"Look, I really didn't see him for all that long. I'm not sure what else I can tell you." She cast her mind back then shrugged. "I think he saw me watching him through the window. He just seemed to fall back into the seat and slammed the door shut. Next thing I know he reversed and pulled out into traffic."

"And is that when you saw his license plate?"

"Yes." She frowned as she thought about it some more. "There was at least one zero and a five in the license plate."

"But you can't remember the rest?"

"No, he drove away pretty fast."

"As in *very* fast?"

In exasperation she threw up her hands. "It's not like I can measure the speed of his acceleration. All I can tell you is, he hit the gas pedal and whipped out of sight. For all I know, he was afraid I would call the cops on him or something, and he didn't want to be seen."

"That makes sense, in an odd way," Cade said quietly. "Let me know if you remember anything else or if you hear any news on your friend." And he hung up.

She stared at the phone in her hand. "Why do you care about Elizabeth?" And yet he'd been keeping abreast of Elizabeth's development the whole time Faith had been here.

The rest of the day passed in a blur as Faith surfed the internet, talked with Elizabeth, went to the cafeteria for a meal, then returning as soon as possible, visited some more with Elizabeth. Faith spoke with the nurses; she spoke with the doctors as much as she could. Several of the nurses spoke English, but none of the doctors appeared to. However, everybody said the news was good, and the longer Elizabeth held on, the better.

Later in the afternoon, the door opened again. She looked up to see Cade.

He gave her a bright smile. "How are you holding up?"

She jumped to her feet, both hands outstretched. He caught her hands and tucked her into a hug. She went willingly. It was amazing how much that single human contact helped when she was under so much stress. She cuddled in close and said, "Thanks for stopping by."

He nodded toward Elizabeth. "She looks to be better." His tone was even.

She searched his gaze to see if he was just trying to make her feel better, but he had seen Elizabeth earlier. "That's what I thought. But her sister doesn't seem to think there's any improvement."

"How often has her sister been here? Every time I see you, you're alone."

She winced. "I know. It's one of those sad facts that, I think, if I wasn't here, Elizabeth would be alone."

"Is there just her sister?"

"And her mother. But honestly they both think she's one step away from the grave and that I'm wasting my time because Elizabeth doesn't know anything."

He slanted a gaze at her in surprise.

She shrugged. "My mother would be the same, I imagine. Instead of wanting to spend every last minute with me, she would be the one to walk away and have the doctors pull the plug."

"That's unusual in a mother," he commented.

"Maybe, maybe not," Faith said quietly. "I think it's their way of dealing with their grief. If they see her again, it's just a massive wrench to the heart."

"And you?"

"I'm not named in vain," she said with a smile. "I'm not religious either," she explained at the questioning look in his eyes. "But I certainly believe in hope. And having faith in the human body and the human spirit. But I think Elizabeth needs to know somebody is here and to know that somebody cares."

Cade nodded. "As somebody who almost died several times on the operating table and was in a coma for several weeks, I can tell you there is truth to that."

She looked at him in astonishment. He smiled and lifted his pant leg. And that was the first time she noticed he had a prosthetic leg. "I had no idea," she said. "Of course I saw your gloved hand, but ..."

He nodded. "Talon is missing a leg and an arm too."

"Bad accident for both of you?"

"You could say that," he said, his voice hard. "Our military truck blew up while we were on a reconnaissance mission. We drove over an antitank land mine. Seven of us were badly injured, and one of our team died."

"Oh, my God."

He nodded. "That's one of the reasons we think we have the right man. As a mockery to the man who died, he took his nickname as a middle name."

"Mouse," she said out of the blue.

He stared at her.

"Remember I overheard you and Talon talking in the hallway."

He turned to look at the hall and nodded. "Normally we're better at keeping information like that to ourselves."

"Well, you don't have to worry. I won't tell anyone."

He smiled. "Thank you. We don't know exactly what's

going on yet."

"But this case is connected to others? You think somebody is connected to that accident?" She was guessing, not sure how taking the dead man's nickname on a car rental application played into this.

He was silent for a long moment; then he nodded and quietly spoke. "We are afraid our land mine accident was no accident. And the person behind it either meant to kill all of us or at least some of us. He successfully killed Mouse. Now it's all too possible he's mocking us by using Mouse's name on the rental."

"He's taking a chance that you guys would even understand the connection ..."

"Exactly. It only occurred to us after we realized several of our family members had been subsequently killed in *accidents.*"

He emphasized the last word, and she stared at him, figuring out what he meant. And then it slowly dawned on her. "So you think the hit-and-run accident Laszlo's father was involved in was a targeted hit?" Her voice rose.

He reached out and squeezed her hand, motioning toward Elizabeth. Instantly Faith shot Elizabeth a quick glance and then turned to look at him. She pushed him lightly toward the door.

He stuck his head out in the hall to make sure they couldn't be overheard, then leaned forward. "Yes, that's what we're afraid of."

She stared at him, her jaw dropping. "That must be a nightmare."

His face, already grim, turned more stone cold than she'd ever seen before. "Not only that, we're also concerned other family members of the seven of us might be targeted."

"Why would he do something like that? And particularly if you seven were already blown up. Wouldn't it make more sense to come back around and take you guys out one at a time instead of taking out your family members?"

He nodded. "Yes, and all of us would welcome a chance to see him one-on-one." His tone was hard, vibrating with anger. "But he's a coward. And he's too busy playing cat and mouse. We think it's a case of serious hate for all of us. And he wants us to suffer in the worst way possible."

"By killing innocent family members?" She had never even contemplated such a thing. And yet, in the twisted mind of a serial killer, it was all too possible. "I'm so sorry. That has got to be tough."

"What's tough is we've just come to this kind of a theory, and now we're tracking down all the supposed accidents over the last two years. And that's opening everybody's barely healed wounds."

She nodded slowly. "I can imagine." She motioned to Elizabeth. "I'm here because I can't bear not to spend every moment with her that she has. I can't imagine having all this ripped open a year from now when I'm still dealing with the grief."

"Exactly." He sighed. "At least Elizabeth was in an accident, and she has a chance of pulling through this. Every day she lives is a day her body has a chance to heal."

"That's what I told her sister."

"And what did she say?"

"She just thinks we are prolonging Elizabeth's pain, and it wasn't fair to her. We should let her die in peace."

Cade shook his head. "In that case, I'd be checking to see if Elizabeth had any life insurance. And who the beneficiary is."

Faith stared at him in horror. "Don't even joke about something like that."

He gave her a hard look. "In the world I come from, that attitude is never without a motive."

Faith shook her head. "The trouble is, I know her sister and mother. They're very similar to my mother. It's why Elizabeth and I became such great friends. All three of them are pessimists. They would never try anything for fear of failing. They would never go after what they wanted because, in their minds, they wouldn't get it. And it would be a typical attitude of all three to let Elizabeth go rather than giving her a chance to fight for her life. They'd say that, even if she did fight, the doctor said it wouldn't work. And that she would die anyway. So why force a body to struggle through all these extra days for nothing?"

"If it was me, I'd want to know somebody was on my side, fighting for me," he said harshly. "My sister was there every step of the way after my accident. When I lost her seventeen months ago, it hit me hard. Even now, just the thought of somebody taking her life, instead of her death being accidental, cuts so hard, so deep."

She reached out and gently stroked his cheek. "Let's hope that's not what happened. You don't have any proof yet. Did you have any suspicion at the time?"

He glanced up and shook his head. "No, they told me that it was a car accident. I was just coming out of another surgery. My recovery was pretty rough. At the time I couldn't reconcile my grief, and healing was not something my body wanted to do when I was ready to yell at the world for stealing from me the one precious thing I had left." He smiled weakly. "But this is a pretty morbid conversation. I have a couple photos I would like to show you. How about we take this away from Elizabeth? Let's go to the cafeteria for half an hour."

She smiled. "I'm game. Let me just grab my bag." Instinctively she repacked all her stuff, including her laptop, and collected her coffee cup, which she tossed in the garbage. With her space clean again, she walked over to Elizabeth, bent down and kissed her on the cheek. "I'll be back." And she turned and strode out, Cade at her side.

CADE WASN'T EXACTLY sure why he'd told her the details of what they suspected. He wasn't normally a talker. And it wasn't that he trusted her or didn't trust her. He didn't know her. And that was what made this all very unusual. Still, as he walked at her side, he didn't see anything not to like. She had brunette hair cut into a bob with a bit of a curl to it. He kind of liked it short and sassy. Must be easy to care for. Considering the type of job she had, it would make her life easier, he was sure.

He wondered about a woman who made it as a commercial pilot. He loved it. She had pushed for what she wanted and had achieved it.

As they entered the cafeteria, he motioned toward the same table they'd been at before by the window. "How about over there?" He nudged her toward the table. "I'll grab coffee."

She smiled at him and headed to claim their place. He walked down the line and poured two cups of coffee, paid for them, snagged a couple muffins as an afterthought, dropping more money in the cashier's hand, then turned and left. He threaded his way through the tables and sat down beside Faith.

She reached out for the coffee and eyed the muffins. "You bought two?"

He nodded. "One for you and one for me," he confirmed and realized he made the right decision when she snatched one off the plate and quickly unwrapped it.

"I'm not sure if it's because I'm sitting here doing nothing, but I'm hungrier now than I seem to remember being in weeks."

"It's better than not eating," he said. "Grief can have very debilitating effects on the psyche. Food helps to nourish the body and to heal the emotions."

"I don't know if that's true or not," she said, her mouth full of muffin, "but it sounds right."

He laughed and reached for the other muffin, cut it in half and buttered it.

She stopped midbite, looking at the butter. "I didn't even see the butter."

He opened up the second pat of butter, reached for the part of the muffin still on the table in front of her and buttered it for her.

She grinned at him. "You're definitely a keeper."

The phrase startled him. He knew that term from Mason's group. But there was no way she would know it. And there was no way he would tell her about it. It had been a running joke among the SEALs for a long time. The trouble was, there were still enough people who tried to get close to Mason, just in case some of that romantic fairy dust ended up on them. Mason's unit was well known to have been struck by Cupid. Every one of them had found an incredible partner and were still together, even after all this time. And sure, it wasn't all that long, but, in the military, sometimes a weekend was a long relationship.

"I don't know about that," he said lightly. "But you're easy to please."

She chuckled. "When I'm hungry, all you have to do is feed me."

"I'll remember that."

He smiled at her, loving the way her chocolate-brown eyes lit up with a warm glow. There was just something nice about her. And there weren't a whole lot of nice girls in his life. There were a lot of women he liked, but Faith was the type of girl he would call *all-American*. She was full of life, strong, walking with a purpose and a surety that he really appreciated. Self-confidence was so sexy. All these women so busy getting Botox injections and their hair just perfect and needed to wear layers of makeup, failing to understand that sexiness came from within.

Although he suspected Faith wouldn't understand what he had to say about this. She might not see herself the way he saw her. Right now, as her bangs drooped slightly to the side, he could see the lines on her face from the lack of sleep having taken its toll, along with the worry and the grief. All of it affecting the shoulder slump and the lack of color in her cheeks.

"You should go for a walk outside every chance you get," he said. "The fresh air would do you some good."

She nodded. "I'd love to, but every time I leave Elizabeth, I feel guilty."

He nodded. "And, if something happens while you're not there, you'll feel terrible. But what she wouldn't want is for you to waste away at her bedside because you didn't look after yourself when she was incapable of helping you."

"No, she wouldn't be happy with that." Muffin gone,

Faith bundled up the wrapper, tossed it on the tray and pulled the coffee cup closer.

He loved the protective way she snuggled up to the coffee, as if she desperately needed it. When she leaned closer and took a deep sniff of the aroma drifting up from the cup, he chuckled. "A coffeeholic by any chance?"

"Absolutely. I think it's a basic requirement for being a pilot too."

"Understood. In the military we had to go sometimes twenty-four to forty-eight hours without any rest." He was remembering some of the worst missions of his life. "It seemed like, if we couldn't inject coffee, we'd never get through another hour."

She nodded. "I've done flights from San Francisco to Singapore, Vancouver to London. I've been on routes to Dubai and summers up to Iceland. The longer flights are just deadly. Even though we're supposed to sleep in between, it doesn't mean you can. Just because you have four hours of downtime doesn't mean your body can shut off like that."

He chuckled. "Same for us. If you're on watch, there is no way you can close your eyes, not even when your watch is over and you have two hours to grab. Often it would take fifteen to thirty minutes to just unwind enough to go out. Some of our unit learned to shut it all off and could drop to sleep, as if they had been unplugged. I was never one of those guys. I was always restless, could never quite manage that complete-silence thing. Mouse, now he couldn't sleep at all. He would need dead silence. And I have to admit, we often bugged him about it. Just when he was starting to fall asleep, we'd make a loud sound that would wake him back up, and he had to start the relaxation process all over again."

He chuckled at the memory. "But he was a good kid. He

was younger than all of us, but he was a real brain. A wizard with electronics. Picked up anything electrical real fast. But he wasn't quite the same at sharpshooting and strategy. The military is hard on people who have weaknesses. We used to tease him a lot. Of course, then we teased everybody."

"I'm sure he realized you loved him anyway," she said reassuringly. "No matter what kinds of things you guys were put through, I understand the brotherhood of being in a unit like that. It would be very special."

He nodded. "Even now, after the accident, after all the many surgeries, we're still in this together." His voice hardened. "And speaking of which, I brought the photos." He pulled them out of his pocket and laid them on the table in front of her. "These are the same guy but with different looks. Could you take a good look and see if you recognize him?" He unfolded the papers and stretched them out flat in front of her.

CHAPTER 8

FAITH STARED AT the photos, feeling the same horrible fear that had clenched her throat when she'd seen the man the first time. She reached a hand to cover the top portion of his face like a hat and nodded mutely. "It's definitely him." She raised her gaze and stared at Cade. "Who is he?"

"According to the paperwork, he's John Smith."

She stared at him and frowned. "Seriously?"

His tone dried as he nodded and said, "According to the paperwork."

She sat back. "And do we believe the paperwork?"

"Hell no." He tapped the photo. "If you look at the other pictures, you'll see him without the beard and the thick eyebrows and a different haircut."

She quickly leaned forward again and shuffled through the pages on the table. He really had a chameleon appearance and managed to look different in each one. "Wow, I didn't think disguises worked quite like they say in the movies."

"They don't. But every once in a while you get someone who does well with them." He tapped the one she'd seen first. "And considering that he was seen here in this disguise, and you saw him in a variation of this back in Santa Fe, he probably no longer looks like this at all."

"Is it just makeup and hairstyles, or is there plastic surgery involved?" She glanced up at Cade to see him shrug.

"I don't know yet. It's possible he has a skill for disguise. It's also possible he was military trained for undercover work. We all have a certain amount of training in hiding our appearance. You just work with the basics and keep switching it up and switching it down."

"So now that you have a photo of him, any chance of catching him?"

He gave her a grim smile. "We hope so. But there's no way to know yet." He stacked the papers together and folded them back up. "We have scanned these and sent them off to various people we know who can help. With any luck, he'll be spotted somewhere."

She frowned. "Somewhere, as in Santa Fe somewhere?" She had to guess.

"It's possible he's still there. But I'm not sure about that."

She glanced around the cafeteria. "I thought I would be off work this weekend, but I have a couple flights scheduled. The doctors told me this morning that Elizabeth could be like this for weeks."

"That's tough. And you have to carry on with your life."

She nodded. "I don't want to leave her though."

"Leave her and then come back. That's the only answer. Maybe by then there'll be a change. Unfortunately some people are in a coma for a long time. We're talking years."

She winced. "I know. I just can't imagine that as a future for Elizabeth. She was always so vibrant."

"Keep that in mind. Let the doctors do their thing and trust in the system. Trust in your friend to fight with what she can fight with, and let go when it's time to let go."

"I know, but it's hard."

"You haven't been here very long yet. Are you staying a few more days?"

"Just a couple I think. When the doctor told me this morning that it could be weeks, I realized I wouldn't be able to stay the whole time. I still have to work for a living," she confessed. "The best thing I can do is spend some time with her now and get more time off to come back."

"That's a good idea." He stood. "Do you want to go back to her room or go back to your hotel now?"

She sighed. "Now that they don't expect her to die in the next twelve hours, it feels like a gamble to leave. The doctor did sound so much more positive, as if she had stabilized but still has a lot of healing to do and needs to pull out of the coma. But because of the drug inducement, they won't give her that chance for quite a few more days."

"And maybe that's a good thing too." He gave her a smile and said, "I'll speak with you later." And he walked away.

Faith walked back to Elizabeth's room and sat down again. She could see Elizabeth had found some sort of a new level. Her face was calm, smooth, as if she had slept easily. She still didn't move or shift in any way. But then how much did one move when in a coma?

The nurse walked in then and smiled. "Just to let you know, the doctors have reduced the drug dosage. We'll see if there's any change in her condition. We should know more in the next day or so."

Faith smiled and nodded. At the same time she was terrified. Was this good or bad?

The door opened again, and she looked up in surprise to see Mary walk in. But it was an angry Mary. Instinctively Faith's back stiffened as she prepared for a fight that she hadn't expected to have.

"Why are you still here?" Mary asked quietly.

Faith raised her eyebrows. "Elizabeth is my friend. I wanted to stay and see how her condition would develop."

"She should have passed already." Moodily Mary walked to the foot of her sister's bed and stared down. "I don't know why she hasn't."

"Because she has improved," Faith said impulsively. "The nurse just said they're reducing the drugs to see if she comes out of the coma."

Mary shot her a look. "You've been talking to them?"

Unsettled Faith sat back and nodded. "Whenever they come in and talk to me," she said. "Obviously I don't go speaking to the doctors beyond any kind of concern as a friend." She wasn't sure Mary believed her though. There was a sharp assessment in her gaze. "Don't be so quick to rush Elizabeth to the grave. The doctors seem to think she has a much better chance now. They did say she could stay in a coma for several days to weeks, and there was no way to know when she'd pull out, but they were hopeful she would pull out."

Mary turned her gaze back to her sister and shook her head. "If she's in a coma that long, it's not good. She won't recover afterward either. Better for her not to recover."

"How can you say that?" Faith jumped to her feet, her voice loud.

"I can say that because I'm her sister, and I know what she'd want. And she wouldn't want to be this frozen vegetable in a bed for the rest of her life."

Faith bit back the words hovering on her lips. She didn't know if this was just Mary being negative, as she knew Mary could be, or if she really believed that. "I don't think it's fair to decide that that's what Elizabeth will be or what her future will be. The doctors are hopeful. That makes me hopeful."

"Hope doesn't put food on the table or bring satisfaction in the morning after a good night's sleep. Hope is nebulous. Hope is something you can't measure, you can't count on. It's just a cover-up for the reality of what we have to live with." Mary bit her tongue. "I called you so you'd have a chance to say goodbye. I wasn't expecting you to move in." She turned on her heels. Before she walked out the door, she said, "I want to talk to the doctor myself." And she was gone.

Hurt, and not sure what to do about it, Faith sat down on Elizabeth's bed and stroked her friend's fingers. "Oh, Elizabeth. What do we do about family? I really need you to wake up and show some signs of improvement so we can get your sister to feel a little more positive about your condition. I would hate to think there was anything going on here that would hurt you. And I can't stay here the whole time and fight for your cause. But I want to."

She bowed her head for a long moment, feeling the pain, the regrets for time not spent together, phone calls not made. She knew Elizabeth understood. She'd been busy too. But, at this moment, it just seemed so hard to face a future without her best friend.

She continued to stroke her fingers and then realized Mary was likely to cause a fair bit of trouble for her too. She didn't know if they could kick her out as she was only a friend, not a family member. And she didn't know why Mary would do something like that, unless it was because she was afraid Elizabeth's condition was being affected negatively by having Faith there. So far, it had only been a positive change.

But sure enough, when the door opened a few moments later, the Norwegian behind Mary had a sharper tone to his voice. Faith turned to look at Mary standing triumphantly in the doorway. The doctor spoke rapidly. And he motioned to the door. Then he turned around and left.

She stared after him, struggling to understand, when one of the nurses came around the corner and said, "You've been asked to leave." Her gaze flicked to Mary and then back again.

"And it's something I have to do? You know I've only been sitting here, keeping Elizabeth company."

The nurse nodded. "I know that. But the hospital has rules. And family members do have control in this situation."

"Even if it's not in the patient's best interests?"

The nurse nodded. "I'm sorry."

Heartsick and devastated, Faith stood, leaned over and kissed Elizabeth's cheek gently. She turned, picked up the rest of her belongings, packing them in her bag, and stepped outside. She didn't bother looking at Mary. It was obvious Mary didn't want anything to do with Faith.

Changing her mind, she turned. "So if your sister dies, who gains from her death?"

Mary stiffened in anger.

"If I were you, you shouldn't make it look like anything you did hastened Elizabeth's death," Faith said, her own anger reaching through her voice, even against her best efforts to stop it. "Elizabeth deserves a chance at life."

"I'm her sister. I know what's best for her," Mary snapped. "You're not welcome here."

"You don't want me here, but Elizabeth does. The fact that you've already written her off and probably made funeral arrangements, waiting for her to kick the bucket so you can take her house and her car, is an entirely different issue. But if she dies because of this, I'll be looking into legal action against you."

With that last parting shot, Faith turned and walked out of the hospital. She could hear Mary sputtering behind her, but, at times like this, it was often hard to know what to say. And truth was, Faith was a little ashamed of her own actions. But she was hurting from Mary forcing her out of the hospital, away from Elizabeth's side.

Distraught, she headed back to her hotel room.

When she got there, she remembered Laszlo. She sent Cade a text. **Can Laszlo find out if I'll be allowed back into the hospital?**

Her phone rang immediately. "What are you talking about?" Cade's voice was sharp.

She told him what had happened. "I don't know if Mary wants Elizabeth to die, or if she's jealous of the relationship between the two of us, but I was just kicked out of the hospital. And honestly I have no idea why. All I was doing was sitting there at her side, talking to her, visiting with her. Just letting her know she wasn't alone."

"They kicked you out? Did they give you any reason?"

"Mary. She was standing in the doorway, smirking, and me being packed up and moved out of the room."

"I'll have Laszlo contact them and find out. Is it better for you to go off and do what we were talking about and come back maybe in a week or two?"

"I don't know. I can hardly think straight right now."

"Understood. Let me talk to Laszlo, and we'll see what we can find out."

"Thanks."

She hung up and went to lie down across the bed.

"Maybe I should leave," she murmured. "But not without a fight."

CADE TOLD LASZLO and Talon what had happened.

Talon frowned. "It's true that family members do have a lot of rights." He stared off into the distance, quietly speaking. "Does she really suspect Mary of having an ulterior motive?"

"I don't think so, up until now. She was a little worried about it, but Mary is a very negative person. Apparently she's like Elizabeth's mom. From the beginning they thought Elizabeth would die, and anything else was just tormenting and prolonging the inevitable, putting her sister through a lot of unnecessary pain."

"And is that true? That is, is she on death's door?" Laszlo asked.

"She was, according to the doctors. That's why Faith made the trip. But according to Faith and the conversation she had with the doctor earlier, Elizabeth was improving. I don't know that it was the same doctor," Cade admitted. "Obviously there's a language barrier, and maybe Faith didn't understand. But, at the time, she thought Elizabeth had improved tremendously and had much better prospects. But she could be in a coma for weeks. Then a nurse came today and told her that they were lowering the drug dosage to see if they could bring Elizabeth out of the coma. The next thing Faith knew, Mary was there. Faith told her the good news, and now Faith has been kicked out of the hospital."

"But they wouldn't have lowered the drug dosage based

on Faith being there," Laszlo said, "so it's obvious it's in the patient's best interests."

Cade nodded. "But then how is it in the patient's best interests to move the one person who has helped Elizabeth to stabilize?"

"But that's not something anybody can prove," Talon added, "that it was due to her presence. Chances are good they'll say it was the medication, time, whatever, but it won't be because of Faith. It's an unknown in medical terms."

Cade nodded. "But because of the language barrier, we need to get to the bottom of it for Faith's and Elizabeth's sakes."

Laszlo nodded. "I can check in the morning."

When morning came, Cade got up to hear Laszlo in the kitchen on the phone. When he heard Elizabeth's name mentioned, he understood Laszlo was following up on the issues.

He poured himself a cup of coffee, wandered over to the window, wondering about a world where a sister who can't be bothered to sit by her dying sister's bedside is angry because her sister's best friend is doing just that. Was it really because of pessimism, or was it something religious, or was it a wish that the sister would die?

Faith had told him she wondered who would receive Elizabeth's belongings and inherit her estate upon her death, and that was a damn good question. But then he lived and worked with people who'd do a lot for very little gain. And people were people all over the world.

When Laszlo got off the phone, Cade turned to him. "Well?"

"I couldn't get a hold of anybody at the hospital who would talk to me because I'm yet again another stranger. So I contacted the detective. We've helped him enough that he was in a benevolent mood. He called the hospital to get the scoop."

Cade stared at him in surprise. "That was a great idea. Get somebody official involved. So, what happened, according to the detective?"

"Mary said Elizabeth was upset by Faith's presence. Althhough they had been friends, they hadn't seen each other in a long time, and she was worried about Faith's motivation for being there."

Anger sucked at Cade's heart. "That's a shitty thing to do."

Laszlo nodded slowly. "They said that, contrary to those words, Elizabeth had improved. They did reduce the drug dosage, hoping to slowly pull her out of the coma. That doesn't mean she will wake up. It's just then it won't be a drug-induced coma," Laszlo said. "However, the family has priority. And they can stop anybody from seeing a patient."

"Even if it's in the patient's best interests that Faith keep visiting?"

Laszlo nodded. "The detective was curious as to what was going on. He said he didn't really have cause to step in and intervene."

"What about visiting hours? Is Faith completely not allowed to visit?"

"She's not allowed to visit."

The two men stared at each other grimly. They'd been at many hospital bedsides in the last ten years they'd served as SEALs. For their final five years in the navy, the seven had all served in the same unit. They had lost people and had helped each other through surgeries. They knew how important friendship was to pulling through on something like this.

"What could possibly be Mary's motivation? Because what she's just done has not only hurt Faith tremendously but it's likely to quite badly hurt Elizabeth's prognosis as well."

"It's pretty easy to check. The detective even mentioned it might be something he could take a look into. We just don't have cause."

Cade stared out the window. "It'll break Faith to know she can't go back. Particularly to have left like that."

"That's quite possible, but again she probably needs to be told she can't go back at all."

"She can't enter the hospital?"

"I don't think they can stop her from doing that. She's not allowed to go to Elizabeth's room."

"So she can sit out in the hall?"

"For the moment, until Mary decides to cause a stink about that too. And that's something Faith needs to consider. What benefit will it be for Elizabeth if Faith upsets Elizabeth's sister any further?"

Cade pulled out his phone to check the time. It was just after seven in the morning. He sent a text to Faith. **Are you up?**

The response was slow to come, but he did get a yes within a couple minutes. He hit Dial and waited for her to connect on the other end. As soon as he heard her voice, he said, "Laszlo contacted the hospital, got an update on Elizabeth's condition and learned Mary has requested that you not be allowed back into Elizabeth's room. Mary says you've had a detrimental effect on Elizabeth's condition. The doctors don't necessarily agree with that, as Elizabeth has definitely improved in the last several days. And, yes, they have reduced the drug dosage and are slowly pulling her back out of the coma. We had to go through Laszlo due to the language barrier, and he's got even less of a connection to your friend, so we spoke to the same detective we've been dealing with on our case. The thing is, the family does have the right to keep you out. And that has been Mary's request, so you're not allowed back in Elizabeth's room—at all." He heard her cry of pain and added in low a tone, "I'm sorry."

"Why would she do something like that?" Faith cried out. "All I ever wanted was to make Elizabeth feel not so alone, give her something to fight for, so she would heal."

"I don't know. And I don't know if Mary has an ulterior motive and wants her sister dead, or whether she's just jealous."

"She was always jealous of me," Faith said sadly. "But I don't know why. She didn't have the relationship with her sister because she didn't give a damn. And she still doesn't give a damn because Elizabeth's lying in bed all alone, and now I can't even go see her." Without warning, Faith broke into quiet sobs.

Cade got up and walked over to the window again, "Hey, I know this is hard. There's no guarantee Elizabeth'll make it one way or the other. I'm sorry you can't go back and see her. You need to head to work, see if you can return in a couple weeks. If Elizabeth does wake up, she has the right to say you're allowed to come in and out. The patient overrides the family if she can speak for herself. Unless there's an obvious detrimental reason to keep somebody away. If the patient really wants you there, I don't think the doctors will stop you."

"But Elizabeth would have to know I was there and that I cared enough to come over and stay with her and that her sister stopped me from coming. And nobody'll tell her. I know Mary certainly won't."

"I'm sure we can get the message to her somehow. But right now, she needs to let her body do what it needs to do. So maybe pack up, head home and return to work. Keep checking in. You can always get an update on her condition, and, when Elizabeth wakes up, I'm sure we can get a message to her somehow."

He listened to her mumble her thanks. Then she hung up.

He stared out the window, wondering why the world was so cruel.

"I gather she didn't take it well?" Laszlo said from behind him.

Cade turned, pocketing his phone. "No. But then, if that was you in a hospital, I wouldn't take it well either."

The two men shared a look. They'd both been there, both knew how important having other people around was to their healing. "We have to find a way to get a message to her. When she wakes up, she can override her sister's intentions."

"That much I'm sure the detective would be happy to do. It's just a quick stop for him, and it would make a world of difference to Faith, and ultimately to Elizabeth."

Laszlo pulled his phone out and dialed while Cade watched, a frown forming on his face. He didn't understand the Norwegian flying around the room. And just as suddenly it stopped. Laszlo put his phone away his lips hard as he gave Cade a fierce grin. "The detective is going to talk to the doctors and make sure they contact him if Mary tries to get them to pull the plug. They can't do more, but given that Mary's behavior is hard to understand, even the medical team say they've seen it before, she has stabilized a lot since Faith was there."

"Good," Cade said with a hard nod. "Maybe we can do something to intervene at that point."

"The detective will let us know what our options are at that time." He crossed his arms over his chest. "Let's hope it doesn't come to that. Legally, we don't have much ground to stand on. He did check into Mary's background but there's nothing to say she's deliberately trying to hurt her sister."

Cade nodded but he couldn't help but think of all the injuries he and his friends had sustained. What if there'd been a Mary in any of their lives? Would they still be here?

CHAPTER 9

FIVE DAYS LATER Faith finally felt like she was back on more normal ground. Since leaving Norway, her life had been one up and down emotional ride. To know Elizabeth was still in a coma was painful. At least she was alive. Faith had implored the hospital to let her come back for a visit and had received the standard rules—until Elizabeth was released from intensive care, visiting hours would be allowed for family members only. And it would take the family's permission to allow Faith to see Elizabeth. Seeing those words written down had been painful.

She felt like she was letting Elizabeth down. Who would fight for her if her own family was against her? And yet Faith was at a loss as to what to do. As long as Elizabeth was still hanging on, there was a chance she would recover. And the doctors hadn't said anything either way, but Faith knew, the longer Elizabeth was in a coma, the more problems would develop later.

Back to work after having missed a few days like she had, Faith was in a frenzy of adjustments, long schedules mixed up, broken sleep, a rinse-and-repeat system.

She woke up in her own bed and lay there for a long moment. "Oh, Elizabeth, would you please wake up?"

She'd taken to talking to her friend all the time. In the silence of her bedroom, she wondered if it was possible for

Elizabeth to hear and to connect this far away. Faith wanted to believe it could happen, but that didn't make it so.

She pushed herself up and leaned against the headboard. She had the next three days off. And they were a welcomed three days, that was for sure. She picked up her phone to check for messages, then checked her email. There'd been nothing new from Cade. Why would there be? She was no longer over there, and she didn't have a clue where he was. Then again, why would he care about staying in touch?

Without allowing herself to second-guess why, she sent him a quick message. **Are you still in Norway?**

She was stunned when she got an almost instant reply. **No, back in Santa Fe. Where are you?**

She laughed. *Talk about a global world.* **I'm home in bed.**

Alone?

Her breath caught in the back of her throat as she read that. Why was he asking that? Because he was interested? Or something else altogether? Frowning, she answered, **Yes.**

Want to meet for breakfast?

She froze. "Yes, I do," she said out loud to the room. She quickly sent him an affirmative reply, asking him where he wanted to meet. After a moment of thinking about it, she added, **Do you have any updates?**

No, but we can discuss this over breakfast. His next text came through with the name of a popular breakfast restaurant.

She frowned and replied, **How about Nonny's instead?**

Thirty minutes?

Sounds good.

She hopped out of bed, feeling better than she had since she had heard about Elizabeth's accident and headed for a quick shower. She blew dry her hair and dressed. Walking outside with her keys in her hand, she unlocked her car, hopped in and drove the short distance down to her favorite coffee shop.

It wasn't really a breakfast place, more a coffee shop, but she'd heard the menu had been changed, so maybe it had more breakfast options now. But maybe Cade had already had a big breakfast and was just looking for a coffee.

She walked in, finding him already sitting there. He glanced up and smiled. There was something about the caring in that smile of his that made her feel as if he were welcoming her home.

In a greeting that was as natural as it was surprising, Cade stood and opened his arms. Even more surprising, she stepped into them and hugged him back. After a moment he released her and looked in her eyes. "How are you really feeling?"

She smiled. "I'm okay. I can't get any news on Elizabeth. Mary won't answer my emails, and the hospital won't talk to me. I can phone the reception desk and get an update. But that's about it. And so far the only updates are that there's no change in her condition."

He motioned at the chair for her to sit down. She sat across from him, surprised to see the restaurant wasn't very busy.

"It's nice right now," she said, glancing around. "Usually it's a lot busier than this."

"We're in between normal mealtimes."

She glanced at him in surprise and checked her watch. "Well, it is eight-thirty. I think that's normal for breakfast."

He chuckled. "It's Sunday morning. Breakfast is usually much later on a Sunday."

She smiled at him. "That's true. But I've always been an early riser. That hasn't changed with the traveling I do."

"I imagine your world consists of a lot of traveling," he said. "As a pilot you have to be going nonstop most days of the week."

"Indeed, I do."

The waitress arrived just then, bringing her a fresh cup of coffee.

She smiled. "May I have a menu, please?"

The waitress disappeared and returned a few moments later with two menus and handed both of them one. "I'll give you both a moment to review the menu, and then I'll return for your orders."

She took a look at hers, muttering, "I'm starving."

"That's a good sign," he said. "When you're a busy person, you need fuel."

She lowered the menu slightly and looked at him. "Do you normally live a crazy-busy life too?"

He shook his head. "I used to," he admitted. "That was before the accident. For the last couple years, it seems like just the effort of getting out of bed and doing my therapy and mandatory exercises are all I could do."

Her gaze sharpened as she considered that. "I've never been seriously ill or in a bad accident," she said quietly. "I can't imagine what you went through. I've had friends who have had long recoveries. A girlfriend of mine had breast cancer when I was in flight school. She had to drop out for the chemotherapy treatments, which were too much. She got another three years of life, and that was it. What she went through was brutal." She watched the look of pain cross his face. "Regardless of why you're in the hospital, the recovery from the physical insult has to be difficult, not even dealing with the emotional and psychological traumas."

He nodded. "One of the men who was in the accident with me is in the hospital right now for more surgery. I'm glad I can be here for him."

She nodded. And then in another unexpected mood, she reached across and squeezed his fingers. "Hopefully he'll be just fine."

He smiled at her, his fingers sliding across hers to hold her hand in a grasp that spoke of more than just friendship. There was both understanding and compassion in that grasp. And also tenderness. She wondered about that. It had been a long time since she had met any man who seemed to have a soft center. She loved the alpha heroes of the world but hated it when they were raw to the core. Everybody needed a soft inside. It was one thing to see a man strong and battle ready, but you also wanted him to have a soft touch, like when dealing with a puppy and a baby.

And she'd seen enough of both sides to know which one she preferred. Without that softness, a man turned hard and ugly over time. One always had to keep reaching inside and filling in that gap with joy and tenderness. And she was grateful Cade appeared to have a bigger soft touch than a lot of other men.

"What about your reason for going to Norway?" she asked. "Did you get any resolution to that accident?"

His face turned grim, and he dropped his gaze to their hands, reaching with his other hand to cup her fingers, stretching them out as if studying her clean white fingernails. "Not really and yet we made some gain. You saw the photos."

She nodded. "Do you think he's still here?" Nervously she glanced around. "You have to understand that man was scary."

He covered the top of her hand with his. "I don't think he's still here," he said cautiously. "But, if it's the same man, then obviously he is comfortable traveling and could be anywhere."

She wriggled her nose. "As long as he's gone from where I am, I don't really care where he is."

He nodded in understanding.

The waitress interrupted them. "Are you ready to order?"

Faith dropped her gaze to the menu and smiled. "I'll have the eggs and toast, please."

"Would you like white or wheat toast with that?"

"Do you have a sourdough?

"Yes, in both white and rye."

Settling on sourdough rye, she waited for Cade to order. She wasn't surprised when he ordered the exact same thing she had. He looked like he could eat. The man had to be six feet, even six two. He was broad across the shoulders, but there was a leanness to him—not a meanness, though there were rough-cut edges to him. But it was as if his body had struggled for a long time and was just holding on.

"How's the hand?"

He glanced down at his gloved prosthetic hand and smiled. He held it up, the fingers moving and shifting at his command. "Technology has come so far," he said, his tone marveling at what he could do. "Badger, this friend of mine who's in the hospital for more surgery, his partner is a prosthetic engineer. She helped pull this hand together for me." He curled the fingers in and reached for the cup of coffee.

She stared at it and smiled. "I hardly even noticed it."

"Goes along with the foot," he said with a smile. But his

gaze was searching, as if to see if that would make a difference.

She stared back at him blandly. "Good for you that there are advancements today that make your life that much easier. Although I imagine a hook and a claw would even be of some help." She held out both her hands. "I broke my right arm once, and it was terrible trying to use my left hand instead. I couldn't write. I couldn't do anything. I was horribly handicapped." She motioned at his hand. "I can't imagine what you went through to get to this stage, but you're there now. I have to admit that I don't think I could do half as well as you are."

Cade laughed. "I think we're all surprised at what we can do when we have to."

She settled back. "And that's the truth, isn't it? We never really know what we're capable of until we get there."

"What will you do now about Elizabeth?"

Faith shrugged. "Keep phoning to see if there's any change. I hope she doesn't die while I'm off on one of my flights. But I have to work for a living, and I certainly can't take six weeks off while she's in a coma. Particularly if I'm not allowed to be at her bedside."

"Have you considered doing an investigation into Mary, as to why she doesn't want you there?"

"Briefly," she admitted. "When something like that happens, all you can think about is the worst-case scenario, that maybe Mary had something to do with her accident, or maybe she'll inherit Elizabeth's estate," Faith confessed. "I know Mary is living with her mother, but I wasn't sure if it was her mother's house or if it was Mary's house, and her mother was living with her."

"And, of course, it's never a nice thing to consider," he

added for her.

She nodded. "The problem is, it's hard to *not* consider something like that. But why would Mary so obviously try to keep me away if that was the case? It makes her look guilty as hell." Faith stared off for a moment, then shook her head. "No, I think it's just her pessimistic attitude. I think she really does think Elizabeth is better off slipping away into the dark night of death rather than fighting to stay here with us anymore."

"Is her life so dark and despondent that she considers everything around her in such a negative way?" Cade asked. "I've been through some pretty shitty times. But I can't say I would ever consider any of my friends needing to just slip away if they were in the same condition. I'd be in there at their bedside, rooting for them to fight and to come back to us."

"Which is exactly what I was doing," Faith admitted. "But apparently I pissed Mary off enough to have them stop me from sitting there."

"Did you ever ask Elizabeth's mother for her opinion?"

"No. I know the mother was pretty angry at me. She didn't want Elizabeth to become a teacher because she figured it would be more torture." At Cade's confused look, she explained. "Elizabeth can't have children. So her mother thought working with children would be like turning the screw, showing her what she couldn't have on a daily basis."

Cade leaned forward. "Or it would give her a taste of all she couldn't have, and she would get the joy of working with the children she loves so much."

Faith's smile was lopsided. "See? You understand. That was my view. I thought spending time with the children would give her something she could never get any other way, but her mother was against it. And she was really angry at me for convincing Elizabeth to become a teacher."

"How did Elizabeth choose teaching?"

"She's always loved kids, so it was a natural choice," Faith said with a laugh. "She was forever regaling me with tales of the kids and what they were doing. I know she loved going to work every day. She loved her kids and worried about them in the evening. She contacted their parents if there was an issue, and she was always there to lend an ear if anybody needed to just talk or she had willing arms if they wanted a hug. She adored her life."

"So then it's all good."

"Maybe. And maybe her mother just didn't like being proved wrong either," Faith said. "I could contact her, but I'm not sure I want to deal with any backlash that might come from her or any additional flak from Mary."

"Good enough. I think it wouldn't hurt for the detective to take a quick look into Mary's background and make sure there isn't anything odd going on."

"I wouldn't mind either," she admitted. "But I certainly can't pay for a private detective, and, if there's no case, you know the police don't have time to dig into this either."

"That's true enough." Cade stared off in the distance. "However, he is a friend of Laszlo's brother, so it might be simple enough to just request it. On the other hand, I won't know until I bring it up. I know the detective did say he would stop in and take a look and speak with Elizabeth if she woke up and let her know you were there for her."

"That's the thing. *If she wakes up.* So far there's no change in her condition."

"And we'll take that as a positive sign," Cade said smoothly. "No change also means no downgrade in her condition."

After that, the two settled into an easy conversation about the weather in Santa Fe and various places across the country where they had both lived. But inside Cade added Faith to the list of people the hitman could target. "When you get home, you need to be super careful." He skated over the full depth of what was going but told her enough to make sure she listened.

"This is your deal, and it's bad," she said gently. "But I doubt he's going to give a damn about me."

"I don't want to take any chances," Cade said. "I'm being cautious. I want you to be too." His gaze held her in place until she nodded. "I will," she said quietly.

Just then the food arrived and offered them a chance to ease up the conversation.

She took one look at the bountiful plate and said, "Yum."

He chuckled. "Glad to see you have a healthy appetite."

"I can always eat," she said comfortably. "My heart goes out to those people who eat and gain weight. That's never been an issue for me." She dug in. There was basically no talking until they were halfway through. She settled back again and smiled up at him. "Sorry, I've been eating so fast. I didn't realize I was so hungry."

"I presume for the last week you buried yourself in work and kept busy so as not to worry about Elizabeth."

She nodded.

"So you probably haven't been eating properly."

"That about sums it up." She studied him. "What about you?" She laid down her fork, picked up a piece of toast and took a bite.

He raised an eyebrow and curled his lips at her. "What

about me?"

"Do you work?"

He shrugged. "Not really."

She stared at him. "Now, in a way, that might be nice."

"And maybe not. While I'm on this mission," he said calmly, "I'm not taking employable work. Before I found any of this out, I was working toward getting a PI license. I've had a couple job offers, one from a military group I know of. They've set up their own private security company out in Texas. I was figuring out if that's what I wanted to do."

She frowned. "Would that be dangerous?"

He shrugged. "Yes, but no more dangerous than anything else I've done in my life so far."

She nodded. "That in itself would offer a measure of comfort because it would be what you were used to."

He looked up in surprise. "That's very insightful of you. So many people think that, when we leave the military, we want to walk away and do something completely different. But it's the job skills I know," he said quietly. "And it's hard to reframe your world with the injuries sustained and to find a way to make a living again. I don't have to work. But I feel better when I am working."

"I can see that. And given your injuries, can you still do the type of work this security company is offering you?"

He nodded. "I would think so. It's my left hand, and that makes things a little easier, as I'm right-handed. Therefore, it's not the hand that I would hold a weapon with. I can drive quite successfully. I can do all those kinds of things. In many ways, I'm not limited at all."

"What about running, exercise? Things like that?"

"My prosthetic leg and foot can switch out for a blade, like you've seen on some runners. And that makes it a little easier, although it takes a bit of effort to remain balanced when it's only one foot involved." He chuckled. "Sometimes I wish I had two running blades because they're so much faster."

She smiled. "I'm really proud of you. You seem to be handling this very well."

"I've done okay," he said cautiously. "But don't get me wrong, there are still times I wake up in the middle of the night with nightmares that just won't quit. I'm being blown to pieces. My friends are being blown to pieces, and it's like an endless loop that never stops."

She winced. "I'm so sorry."

He shook his head. "Don't be sorry. And don't have any sympathy for me. Definitely don't pity me." His words hardened. "I've never been one to worry about what I can't have or can't do. I've always just found a way to do what it is I want to do and to forget about the rest."

"I didn't mean to sound like I pitied you. In fact, it's the opposite. I admire you. And, if you can continue doing the kind of work you do even after your injuries, then that's perfect." She leaned forward, changing the subject abruptly. "Do you still have those photos on you?"

He raised his eyebrows but fished in his pocket and pulled out a folded piece of paper. Smoothing it out, he said, "Just the one."

She continued to eat while she studied the photo. "I know it's the same guy from the car thing. I just wondered if I had seen him anywhere else. It's one of those faces you're sure you would be able to recognize, but, at the same time, he could be so many people."

"I know."

The waitress walked by with a coffeepot. "Would you

like a coffee refill?"

"Yes, please," Faith said with a smile. She leaned back so the waitress could lean across.

When she was done, the waitress stopped and looked at the picture. "Hey, I know him," she said with a frown. "Is he a friend of yours?" Her tone was edgy, as if that wasn't a good thing.

"I wouldn't call him a friend," Cade said cautiously. "Where do you know him from?"

"He was here yesterday. He threw a fit over his breakfast. Said it wasn't cooked right, and it was cold." The waitress shrugged. "You get some customers who are like that. No matter if the same breakfast is served to five different people, you'll always get one person who's just plain miserable about it."

Faith glanced at Cade, then back at the woman. "Any idea who he is?"

The waitress shook her head. "No. And I'm okay if he doesn't come back. And, if he does, I certainly don't want him at my table." She laughed. "But he didn't stiff me on the bill or anything, so that's good. Even paid in cash, so no bouncing check or anything."

"You didn't happen to see what kind of vehicle he was driving, did you?"

She laughed again. "Sure did. It was a Lexus sports car. And I remember it had a seven and a five in the license plate. Beyond that I don't know. I'm almost certain he shot me his middle finger as I stood at the window and stared at him."

"Yeah, he's got that kind of attitude," Faith said. "Thanks."

"Did he do something wrong?" the waitress asked hopefully. "I wouldn't be at all upset to see him behind bars or at least harassed a little bit."

Faith chuckled. "I think he likes to harass other people. He's not used to being harassed."

"Did he still have the beard?" Cade asked.

She nodded. "He did. Looked pretty damn close to that photo." She turned and walked away.

Cade looked at Faith. She looked at Cade. "So, is he still in town?" Faith said in a low voice. "Will you track him down?"

Cade gave her a slow smile. "Oh, hell yeah. Don't you worry. I'll find him."

CADE STOOD IN the parking lot as he dialed Erick. As soon as Erick answered the phone, Cade said, "The waitress here saw our guy yesterday morning."

"What waitress? What guy? And where are you?" Erick asked patiently.

Cade grinned. "Some things never change."

"Nope, they sure don't. You want to slow down and give me the information bit by bit so somebody like me can process it?" he joked.

"I'm at a coffee shop with Faith." He looked around to see Faith standing outside her car on the phone too. He grinned at her, and she smiled. "I pulled out the photo at Faith's request for her to take another look, and the waitress recognized him. Apparently he threw a fit about the food and then shot her his finger her when she stood in the window watching him as he disappeared in the Lexus convertible."

"So Faith had that much right. And that was yesterday?"

"Yes, yesterday morning."

"So, he's probably still in town."

"That's the thought I had. That would be at least ten days apart from when Faith saw him."

"Interesting," Erick said quietly. "We're still coworking all the accidents. But to have this many *accidents* ... There are eight, by the way. That we know of among us, short of hearing anything from Geir. All but Laszlo's father ended up in death."

"Eight family members who may have been attacked to get back the seven of us? Not Geir right? He had no one close he said."

"Yes."

"But Talon said he had nobody close too."

"His best friend from school was walking along in a parking lot and was downed by a hit-and-run driver."

"Another vehicular accident," Cade said softly. "Son of a bitch."

"Yeah, that's what we've come to figure. All the *accidents* were vehicular."

"Shit." Cade stared at the parking lot. "Chances are he won't use the Lexus to hit people with."

"No, not likely. We're tracking down names and looking for other rental vehicles. I did speak to Laszlo. He was on the phone to Norway this morning making arrangements for his father. They have a record of our hired gunman arriving and staying for two nights, then leaving again."

"That makes sense. And we do have a name now."

"Sure, but the name goes nowhere."

"Oh, the waitress did say she remembered two numbers on the license plate."

"Okay. I got that. I'll add that to what Faith remembered, see if we can run that down." His voice took on a distant edge, as if concentrating while he typed on his laptop.

"How's Badger?" Cade asked abruptly.

"Out of surgery. Still not awake yet." Erick's tone dropped. "And Faith's friend was in a car accident too, right?"

"Elizabeth Brown, yes, and no improvement on her either."

"No connection to our case?"

"Not that I can see."

"Good, we've got enough complications as it is."

"All these *accidents* mean we'll have a hell of a time tracking down anything on them."

"I know. And, in all cases, there's no suspect. And that's even more concerning since someone has systematically run down everybody in our lives who matters."

"I don't know about you," Cade said abruptly, "but I can't imagine anybody doing that. I've racked my brain over and over again to figure out who could hate us all so much. I keep coming back to missions. But it's always governments we've helped, overthrowing insurgents we've taken down, not anybody who would hunt us down on a personal level."

"Me too," Erick said wearily. "Same for Talon and Laszlo."

"And Geir and Jager?"

"Jager is still dark. Geir is on his way here."

"Geir is?" Cade straightened, a big grin breaking across his face. "I'm really looking forward to seeing him."

"He was supposed to be here a couple days ago. But he got sidelined in London."

Cade frowned. "Something to do with Badger's issue over there?"

"Maybe. He said he has some more information. He'll tell us about it when he gets here."

"Sure wish people would stop doing that. With all the deaths, I don't think anybody should be withholding information, just in case they never get a chance to share it."

"I hear you. But Geir will tell us when he finally gets here."

"Did Laszlo have anything else helpful to add?"

"No. The detective in Norway has done what he can do. He doesn't have any other lines to tug."

"Right. So what do you want me to handle next?" As he leaned against his car, he watched a black Lexus pull into the coffee shop parking lot. "I'm not exactly sure what this is," he said in a low voice, "but a black Lexus with a soft top just pulled in at the other end of the parking lot."

Cade walked casually past a few vehicles, back to his truck, and then back again as if pacing. He walked a little farther each time, to appear as if he was completely unconcerned about what was going on around him. What he wanted was to check out the license plate.

"Can you see who it is?" Erick asked sharply. "And not be seen doing it?"

Just then somebody tugged on his arm. He turned to see Faith pointing at the vehicle that had just pulled in. He tugged her up close, dropped a kiss on her temple and whispered, "I know. I'm talking to a friend of mine about it."

She squeezed him and nodded.

But he didn't let her go. "Erick, Faith is right here beside me."

"I don't know what the relationship is between the two of you, buddy, but I don't think there was anybody in your life when your sister went down. What you don't want is to give this guy any idea that Faith is part of your world."

Cade immediately dropped his arm and stepped back. He stared down at her. She frowned and looked up at him, reaching a hand to his cheek, whispering, "What's the matter?"

Just then the Lexus turned all the way around the parking lot and parked beside Faith's vehicle. Deliberately Cade turned so his back was to it.

"Faith, is there any way you can take a picture of the driver as he gets out or take a look at him?"

She nodded and deliberately sauntered back to her car and unlocked it, opening the door. She reached in and pulled a Kleenex out from the side. Quietly and very ladylike, she blew her nose. He could see her from the corner of his eye, but not close enough to see if she could view the new arrival.

"Don't forget. We don't want this guy to recognize her either. They've had a falling out already," Erick warned.

"I think the guy just went inside. Why would he come back if the food was terrible?"

"Unless he's waiting for somebody," Erick suggested. "Who the hell knows what's going on?"

"Cade," came the soft whisper.

He spun around to see Faith walking around behind the truck toward him. As she reached him, she murmured, "It's him."

He took a deep breath. "Erick, I'll go in. I need to know who this guy is."

"You be careful. Wait five minutes for me to send somebody as backup."

"Nobody's close, are they?"

"Talon is here, and so is Laszlo. We'll all be there in ten minutes."

Cade pocketed the phone and leaned against the hood of his truck, staring down on Faith. "My buddy is coming along with a couple other guys for backup. I don't know if this guy knows me, but, if he ran down my sister, I suspect it was deliberate, and, therefore, he knows exactly who I am. He may have already seen me here, but I don't want you getting involved. He's already had a confrontation with you."

"Sure he has, but he's also been at this restaurant where he complained. Why would he come back?"

"It's hard to say. Maybe he's had lots of good experiences here, and that was not one of them."

She groaned. "I don't even want to leave because that guy is here. And I feel bad for the waitress."

Cade winced at that. "I know. The waitress is a little bit of a concern."

Just then he watched her come out of the restaurant and head to a vehicle at the far side of the parking lot and drive away.

"It looks like she just got a lucky break because she's leaving," he said quietly, motioning to the woman.

Faith nodded. "But that doesn't get you or me out of this."

He gave her a lopsided grin. "Sweetie, this is what I do. I'm not trying to get out of anything. I'm trying to get in the game. So, I would like you to go home. At least there you'll be safe."

She shot him a look. "I would like the same for you," she said in a dark tone. She headed back toward her car. "Make sure you text me and let me know what happened."

With a huge sense of relief he watched her back out her vehicle and head home. The last thing he wanted was to have her get any more involved. He reached inside his truck and pulled out his baseball cap, tucked it over the top of his head and walked around to the back of the restaurant. He didn't want to be recognized, and there was a chance he'd already been spotted. But he did want to take a photo of the Lexus's license plate. He just wasn't sure how to do that. He was hoping, if he could get far enough away from the windows at the front of the restaurant, he could take a photo without being seen. He pulled out his phone and set it for Camera and casually walked along the back of the parking lot. As he went by, he checked the numbers on the Lexus and realized both women had been correct. What was missing was an *O*. But there was no way to take a photo without somebody seeing him.

He walked all the way to the far side and then headed back around again. This time as he walked past with the phone at his hip, his arm down casually, he clicked the button to snap a photo of the vehicle, taking several photos, just in case the first one didn't work out, then hopped into his own truck and pulled out to the shopping mall on the opposite side. There he parked and sat in the cab, waiting for his backup to arrive.

Soon Laszlo pulled up in a Jeep to the far side of the coffee shop, driving past the Lexus.

As he parked, Cade called him. "He's inside," he said quietly. "Chances are he already knows exactly who we all are."

"What about Faith? Is she still here?" Laszlo asked.

"No. The waitress is gone on her break, or her shift's over because she just left too. She knows Faith and me. Plus the hired gunman in there knows Faith and me and probably you too. What we need is somebody to go inside who he doesn't know."

"We want to flush him out and get the real identity of this guy. For that we'll have to take him down."

"I think we should wait for him and then one of us get into the vehicle with him and see if we can have a *talk*," Cade said.

"I'd say kidnap him and take him somewhere so we don't have to worry about it."

"We can't cross the line here," Cade said. "We don't have any jurisdiction, and we don't belong to any military group or law enforcement group that'll have legal rights to get involved in this."

"We can hardly just let this guy sit in the coffee shop and then leave."

"He's getting company," Cade said urgently. "I'll call you back." Tucking the phone away, he grabbed a jacket.

Cade quickly crossed the road and walked into the back of the coffee shop. With his jacket on and his baseball cap lowered, looking a whole lot older than he had a few years ago, he walked up to the counter and ordered a coffee to go. The two men sat in the far corner. The new arrival was facing Cade, but he didn't recognize him.

Cade grabbed his coffee and headed outside. As he walked out, he went to the right and headed in Laszlo's direction. He held out the coffee for him. "Here, you need this."

"Did you see the new guy?" Laszlo demanded.

"Yes, but I didn't recognize him."

"We need to get his license plate number and run him down."

"I already passed it along to Erick."

Just then Cade's phone rang. He put it on Speaker.

"Cade," Erick said, "I just ran the second license plate. He's ex-military."

Cade's back stiffened. He didn't like this turn of events. "What's this got to do with anything? We were assuming all these *accidents* might have been done by one guy. But what if he hired some of these jobs done?"

"Unfortunately that's all too possible," Laszlo added. "We still don't have a motive. We still don't have any idea how any of this ties into our land mine explosion."

"We're hoping to get a photo ID to confirm who this second man is," Erick continued. "He was a supply clerk in the military. He was kicked out under suspicion of stealing, but nobody could prove anything."

"Stealing what?" But Cade knew. Inside he knew.

"Weapons, and that includes antitank land mines."

"Shit."

With Laszlo staring at Cade, the two realized they had to capture both men. If there was one thing they needed, it was a chance to talk to this pair of guys, the chance to talk to them when they couldn't avoid it.

After a moment both men exited the coffee shop in a hurry. They split to the two vehicles they had arrived in and took off, leaving Laszlo and Cade staring after them.

"Something's up," Cade said to Erick, still on the phone, as Cade raced toward his truck. "They both just ran off."

"Can you each tail them?" Erick demanded.

"Yeah, we're on it." At least Cade hoped so. But the men already had a head start.

Laszlo pulled past Cade, honked once and took off after the Lexus. The Jeep would give it a good run, but that Lexus could outrun it if they were on a flat surface. But there was a lot of traffic, so chances were he wouldn't get that opportunity.

Cade threw himself behind his truck's steering wheel, pulled out behind the BMW the second man had arrived in. It was a rental vehicle. And a high-end one at that. But this guy wouldn't know the area like the first man did, since he had to rent a car. And he was much slower to pick up and head out. That was good with Cade because he could follow him.

He set the GPS on his phone and told Erick, "The GPS is live. Track us. Laszlo has gone off after the other asshole. Don't lose these guys."

"Not an issue. Talon is hopping in his vehicle now too. I'll direct him to the best point as soon as I bring everyone up on the map. You go easy. No accidents allowed for anyone."

"I hear you. Let's make sure we catch these guys."

He tossed his phone on the seat beside him and took off after the second vehicle.

CHAPTER 10

FAITH REALLY WANTED to head home. But knowing this was all going on had left her with an edgy, unsettled feeling. She was in the mall parking lot across the street from the coffee shop when she realized Cade had parked nearby but was no longer visible. She walked up and down the parking lot, watching. She saw the first guy that Cade was tracking come out of the coffee shop with a second guy, and both got in their separate vehicles. Then Cade and Laszlo followed the two vehicles. She wanted in on it but knew she didn't have the skills or the temperament for something like that. She also had no way, outside of Cade, to contact them. She hoped they caught them. She had no clue what was going on, but the one man she knew for sure definitely needed to be taken down.

Sighing, she turned and walked into the nearby market, picked up a few groceries and headed back to her vehicle. Just as she sat down, there was a text from Mary.

You went to the police?

Faith winced. That wasn't exactly how she wanted Mary to find out. Laszlo's detective had probably contacted her. Faith hemmed and hawed over her response, and then sent a text back. **I had to know what my rights were.**

You have no rights. She's my sister.

She's also my friend, and I care about what happens

to her.

If you care about her, stay on your side of the ocean came back the snappy retort.

Frustrated and angry, Faith tossed the phone in her open purse beside her and slowly drove home. She didn't know what was going on in Norway—or even here in Santa Fe—but her world had suddenly flipped. It was more than unsettled and unpleasant. She wanted it all to return to normal, where she could pick up the phone and call Elizabeth, and they could laugh away the hours.

But she couldn't talk to Elizabeth. Mary was making sure of that. Faith was doing her best to give Mary the benefit of a doubt, but Mary was making that harder and harder to come by. And Faith didn't want to have these negative thoughts rebounding in her head all day long. She had to stop the Repeat action of Mary's message playing over and over.

Shaking her head, parked at her apartment now, she pulled the groceries out of her vehicle, locked up the car and headed inside. As she crossed the parking lot toward the main entrance to the complex, a black vehicle raced past her, coming a little too close for comfort. She had been distracted by Mary's words still in her head, but Faith had dashed the last few feet to get away, shouting, "Watch your speed, idiot."

Too bad she didn't get another look at the vehicle, but it was long gone now. She let herself into the apartment building and upstairs to her third-floor apartment. She couldn't afford much more than this one cost, plus hadn't decided where she wanted to live. She hadn't even chosen what city she would like to live in. The world was wide open for her. The last thing she wanted to do was buy into a real estate area that she would end up hating.

She dumped her groceries on the kitchen counter and started to put them away. Her phone rang. She knew who it was. "Cade, what happened after I left?"

"Was that you dashing out of the way in the parking lot?" His voice was terse.

She spun around to look at her front door. "Did you see that? Who just tried to run me down?"

"The guy Laszlo is tailing. He called to say he saw you as he went past."

"I assumed it was an accident."

"I don't think anything's an accident anymore," he said grimly.

"Coincidence?" she offered.

"I'm afraid it was more a case of, *I can get to her any time I want to.*"

She gasped and froze. "Are you saying that was a deliberate attempt to hit me?"

"That was a little too close for comfort. My comfort."

"Well, it was a hell of a lot too close for my comfort too," she declared. "Could you guys take out these assholes, please? They're really mucking up my life."

He gave a surprised laugh. "That's the spirit." And he hung up.

She frowned and put down the phone. It was hardly anything to laugh about. This was just plain ugly. She didn't have anything to do with Cade's nightmare. Although Cade had interfered into hers in a nice enough way, although Mary obviously was pretty pissed off about the whole deal.

Faith put on a small pot of coffee, even though she didn't really want any. She wanted a warm drink, the comfort of the routine. Walking over to her laptop, she turned it on. When it booted up, she checked her emails. There was one from Mary. In it was a long explanation of why she felt Elizabeth was much better off without Faith. The trouble was, it read like an eight-year-old's temper tantrum.

She responded in kind.

Just because you're jealous of the relationship the two of us had and obviously prefer a world where your sister isn't in it, that's no reason to actively hurt other people. Elizabeth and I have always been friends. That has never encroached on your relationship with her. She's a beautiful woman who deserves a chance to live. And, if sitting at her bedside brought her any measure of comfort, I was happy to do it. Being forced away from her room because of your jealousy is madness.

She knew she shouldn't hit Send, but she did anyway. There were some times one should walk away, but there were also times when one needed to make one's position clear. In this case, Faith was worried about Elizabeth's safety in the hands of Mary and their mother. Plus Mary had seriously pissed off Faith.

She got a response a few minutes later and read it.

That's just mean. She's my sister, and I love her. She never understood me, and I never understood her, but our love was always underneath there.

Obviously Mary wouldn't get it anytime soon. Faith typed up her reply email.

So then why would you choose for Elizabeth to not have her best friend there? I wasn't hurting her. Even the doctor said she was more at peace when I was there. So, unless you're helping your sister to an early grave in the hopes of getting her assets or at least your mother's undivided love or some other twisted reason, I suggest you take a very good look at what you created here.

The back and forth continued. According to Mary, it was a kindness, and, according to Faith, it was a travesty. But still Faith could do nothing about it. Mary had set this in motion, and there was no stopping this travesty, unless Elizabeth woke up, or Mary changed her mind. The chances of the latter happening weren't very good. All Faith could do was hope Elizabeth healed enough to come out of the coma on her own.

The longer she stayed under, the harder recovery she would have, and the more time she would need to get back to normal. Depressed, Faith thought about going out for a walk, but remembering that vehicle almost hitting her, she realized there was a good chance somebody was after her. And yet, why? Because she'd seen Cade once or twice? That made no sense. And that just showed how truly psychotic the mess Cade was involved in. And she didn't want any part of it. She was afraid it was already too late. If what Cade had said was true, the serial killer was just proving he could get at Faith anytime he wanted to. Whether she was in the parking lot or not, he knew where she lived.

On that note she got up and locked the front door. She didn't think anybody could break in through the third-floor windows, but it wouldn't be hard to find her name on the panel on the main floor. If somebody was determined to get in her apartment, she knew they would get in. She wasn't a fool. She might have lived with more sunshine and roses than a lot of people, but that didn't make her naive.

At the thought of somebody breaking into her apartment, she examined the lock she had. She didn't have much. One dead bolt and, as far as she knew, that was pretty easy to bypass. Trouble was, she really didn't know if it was or it wasn't.

What she needed was an expert. She sent a text to Cade. **When you get a moment, you want to come by and check out my security? If I'm involved, I want to know I'm safe.**

Frowning, her stomach squeezing uncomfortably, she wandered her small apartment, wondering what she had gotten herself into. Her phone buzzed with a text. It was from Cade.

I'm downstairs. Let me up.

She frowned. He hadn't buzzed the intercom. As she walked over to the intercom button, it rang. She clicked on it and said, "Cade?"

"Yes, let me up."

"How did you find out where I lived?" she asked quietly.

There was a moment of startled silence, and then he chuckled. "Good for you. Suspect everybody. Remember we shared a cab on that first meet? We saw the apartment building then. But also Laszlo saw you dash into this building today, remember? After that it was pretty darn easy to find your name."

She frowned. What he said was plausible. She sighed. "You better not be an ax murderer." She hit the button, cutting off any response to her comment, but she was definitely feeling uneasy. She stood at the open front door as she waited for the elevator door to open. But when the door to the stairs opened instead, she gave a start to see Cade walking toward her.

She frowned at him. "Why'd you take the stairs?" She motioned at his leg. "Isn't it better to take the elevator?"

He gave her a good frown back. "All exercise is good.

And stairs are especially good for the heart."

She shrugged. "Most of the time I'm too damn tired." She pointed him inside the apartment behind her.

"Am I allowed in? Or are you still wondering if I'm an ax murderer?" He grinned.

Her frowned deepened. "It just occurred to me—maybe it's silly—but I really don't know who you are."

His hand went to his back pocket, pulled out his wallet and held it out to her.

She glanced at the driver's license to see the same name she already knew. "But that doesn't tell me anything. It doesn't let me know if you're a good guy or bad guy."

"What brought this on?" he asked curiously.

"I don't know. I'm a little unnerved after that vehicle almost ran me down."

He stepped forward and automatically she stepped back into her apartment. He followed her. She closed and locked the door behind her.

He studied the locks. "You should get a better system."

"I was wondering about that," she admitted, studying the lock on the door. "It never was an issue before."

"It's always been an issue. It's just not one you've been aware of," he corrected. He walked around the small apartment, checking the windows, looking out to see how far a drop it was and if there were any balconies. He turned back to her. "Is there any reason why this guy would know where you live?"

Bewildered, she shook her head. "I have no idea. Unless he wrote down my license plate number from our first encounter—when he almost ran into me on my way to the bank—and followed up that way. I don't even know who he is. Any more than I know who you are."

"That's not quite true," he said calmly. "You know I've only ever been here to help you and to be a friend. I have no reason to hurt you in any way."

Giving in because he was right—he'd been nothing but friendly and helpful so far—she muttered, "That's what any serial killer would say."

At that, a bark of laughter escaped. He grinned and sat down in the living room. "Are you really scared of me?"

She thought the question was flippant, but the look in his eyes was serious, pure, and she realized he was offended. She sat down beside him and sighed. "No, I'm not. I just don't like the sudden turn in my life."

"Anything other than the man who just tried to run you down in the parking lot? And, yes, that was enough to make anybody upset. But did Mary do anything else? Or anybody else do something to you?"

She shook her head. "No, nothing else has happened. Other than the *pleasant* back-and-forth email exchange with Mary earlier today. She explained to me how she doesn't want her sister tortured any longer. But other than that, no."

"Have you contacted the hospital again?"

She shook her head and slid lower on the couch, stretching out her legs to put her feet on the coffee table. "No, I haven't bothered. It's a terrible state of affairs as I just wait and see which way Elizabeth will go."

He reached over and covered her hand with his. His fingers gently slid in between hers, the gesture almost intimate. "I've been at a lot of hospital beds in the last couple years, and it's never a nice experience. It doesn't matter which side of that railing you're on."

She glanced up at him and thought about all the surgeries he'd had and the pain and loss he'd experienced. She squeezed his fingers. "I'm sorry."

He slanted a sideways grin at her. "It's okay. At least I'm alive."

The sincerity in his voice reassured her. Although he'd been through a lot, he at least was grateful for having the life he did have.

"Did you need to chase him?"

"Well, if I didn't, he'd probably realize we put a tracker on his vehicle. He had to know we were there at the coffee shop, and he'd know there was a good chance we'd stop him and put an end to this right away. The tracker is just a backup, so we have some idea of where he's going." Cade shrugged. "Then Talon took over tracking the Lexus, which freed up Laszlo to track the BMW, so I could come here. Laszlo followed the BMW to a hotel at the airport, where Laszlo's now in the parking lot, working his laptop, checking on the hotel's guest list."

"No photo?"

"Not yet. We need a reason to get law enforcement to give us one off the city cameras. And there really isn't any reason we can give them that's viable," he admitted. "Being connected to a suspected serial killer is not enough. We don't know anything about this guy. He could be a friend or an innocent business associate."

"Do you believe that?"

He gave her a shake of his head. "Hell no."

"Aren't you supposed to be helping them?"

He nodded. "I needed to check on you first, to see if you knew anything. And I do have to leave again now."

She sighed. "Of course you do."

"Do you not want me to?"

Determinedly she straightened her shoulders and sat up.

"No. I know you need to catch these two guys and to figure out what the hell is going on. I'll be fine here."

"When do you fly out again?"

"Not for three days."

He frowned. "Have you got any plans for the rest of to-day?"

"I would normally do some shopping," she muttered. "But I'm not so sure now."

"I know you probably don't want to do this, but it would be a good idea if you kept me aware of where you go."

"Meaning, if I go to the mall, I'm to send you a text saying that's where I am?"

He nodded. "Just be safe."

She didn't even know what to say to that. "How does that keep me safe? It'll be the one time I don't check in that you won't have any idea what's happened to me."

"Exactly."

Just hearing him speak like that had her mind freeze up in fear. "Is that likely to be an issue? I'm not sure how to feel about that."

"Otherwise stay here. I'll pick up something for dinner and come back." He jumped to his feet, checking his watch. "You don't have to decide now. Just let me know what you're up to." He headed to the front door, opening the bolt. "Lock up behind me. I'll be back tonight. And maybe you can check on upgrading your security. At least adding another dead bolt."

Again she was torn. She wanted him to return, but, at the same time, she was worried. Was she getting too close to him? And would that be a problem? He seemed like a nice man, but, with the things that had happened today... "I'll let you know what I decide," she hedged.

He grinned and nodded. "Good enough. Just remember to stay safe." And, with that, he stepped out into the hall, checked both directions and turned back to her. "Have you ever had a problem with any of your neighbors?"

Surprised, she automatically glanced down the hall. "No. I hardly even know any of them. Not sure I can place a name to anybody here."

"How long have you lived here?"

"Two years. But I come and go without regular hours, so it's kind of hard to strike up a relationship."

He nodded. "Understood." He lifted a hand in a wave, turned and headed the opposite way he came.

"Wait. How come you're not going down the stairs this time?"

He continued to walk but turned so he was walking backward. "I want to check out the other stairwell." He flashed her a bright smile, turned and kept on walking.

She stayed in the doorway until he disappeared into the opposite stairwell. The only reason to check out the other stairwell was to check out the other exit.

And that meant he was still in protector mode, looking to see if anybody else could get in or get out of this building. She should be happy, but, at the same time, he made her incredibly nervous.

She stepped back inside, closed the door and locked it. The single dead bolt would not be much of a deterrent for anybody. He was right; she needed to get another bolt, and, even so, it wasn't enough. But it was something.

She sat down on the couch, not a clue as to what she wanted to do now. When she got up this morning, she'd been delighted to have the time off. But now she felt lost and alone. Particularly after Cade had left.

There was something about him that was just so much more than most men she knew. That self-confidence, determination, sense of power around him was really attractive. And then there was that soft core. How could she possibly have thought he'd have been a bad guy? There was no way. It wasn't part of his makeup. And now that she finally reconciled her earlier uncertainty, she realized she really did want to have dinner with him.

She picked up her phone and sent him a quick text. **Bring Chinese.**

CADE RACED DOWN the second stairwell, putting his artificial lower leg to the test. There were still some pressure spots as he landed each and every time, but it was doing much better than he expected. He'd been looking forward to trying out this leg in a real-life situation, where he needed to trust it to be there for him.

As he went down the stairs, he automatically checked for exits and access points, keeping an eye out for any cameras. But there didn't appear to be any. How was that even possible in today's day and age?

Outside in the parking lot, he walked to his truck and hopped in. As he turned on the engine, his phone rang. It was Laszlo.

"Can you join me at the airport hotel? The second guy has gone to his room and has stayed there so far."

"On my way," he said. As an afterthought, he added, "Any follow-up on the Lexus?"

"Talon is still behind him," Laszlo said. "Erick is running point. The thing about the Lexus, if it's still our bearded guy, John Smith, he appears to be heading straight for Texas."

"Why Texas?" Cade's mind raced to fill in the answers. The only ones he came up with were not good. It sounded like Levi might be getting company. "Anybody have any connection with Levi and his group? A lot of men work and live there at the compound. Some we know. Some we don't. You know there'll be at least some connections between our team and theirs. There always is. Tell Erick to send a warning to Levi and Ice. And maybe give Levi the coordinates so they can keep track of them too via their satellite link. It never hurts to have a welcome party on the other side."

"Will do. Just get your ass in gear and get over here."

Cade pulled out into traffic, and his phone went off again. Thinking it was Laszlo, he reached for it, only to find a message from Faith. He chuckled at the Chinese order. He didn't have time to respond but kept driving toward the airport. He'd answer her later.

The traffic was brutal, but he made it in about twenty minutes. He pulled up beside Laszlo's Jeep.

The two of them exited their vehicles and stood in the parking lot for a few moments before Laszlo said, "The BMW driver returned just ahead of me, went to reception and took the elevator up to his room. Hasn't come back down. Yet."

"Do you know what floor?"

"Eighth."

"Should we pay him a visit?"

Laszlo grinned. "Absolutely." The two men went into the front reception area and took a step to the right where the bank of elevators were.

"So, considering this place is so damn crazy, full of people, do you think the timing was intentional?" Cade asked Laszlo.

Laszlo chuckled. "Maybe. It's a busy place most times, being so close to the airport. Plus an airport shuttle came in about ten minutes ago. I was hoping you'd get here in time that we'd be able to sneak in through the confusion."

"There will still be cameras."

"Of course. But some things are instinctive. Including turning our faces against the cameras. As are things like this." Laszlo pulled out a hotel room key.

"Wow. Glad the military trained you for something."

"Not only did they train me for something, but they trained me well," Laszlo said in a hard voice. "The trouble is, after all our training in the navy, what are we to do with those special skills now that we're private? And I certainly don't want to lose my abilities, so I have to stay in practice somehow."

They started up the stairs. Eight floors would be hard on Cade's leg, but he was damned if he would say anything.

"Do you want to take the elevator?" Laszlo asked.

He shook his head. "No, I'll be fine."

The two men continued up the stairs. Laszlo's steps slowed naturally, with Cade holding back.

Laszlo opened the stairwell entryway to the eighth floor. "It's clear," Laszlo said quietly.

Cade walked through the hall. It was empty besides Laszlo, a good ten feet ahead of him. Cade followed at a slower pace as Laszlo made it to the room number they were looking for. Cade didn't ask questions about how Laszlo knew that information or what kind of a hotel card he had. Cade wouldn't put it past Laszlo to swipe a master. Other than that, it was pretty damn easy to get in anyway, but Laszlo had skills like nobody else Cade knew.

It was an odd thing, but everybody had certain definitive *gifts* they had picked up and not necessarily while in the navy. Some had learned them growing up. They were all gifted. And this was definitely one of the ones Laszlo was gifted at.

As soon as Cade reached him, Laszlo had opened the door and entered. Cade slipped in behind, turned and locked the door. The man was on the phone, talking, and didn't even hear them come in. He turned, caught sight of them, tossed his phone down and roared, "What the hell?"

Laszlo took up a spot by the glass doors and smiled. "Not to worry. We just want to have a talk."

The well-dressed man warily looked from one to the other.

Cade smiled. "Particularly want to talk about your bearded companion from the coffee house an hour ago. We know him as John Smith"

The man held back any expression, but a flicker of awareness crossed his face.

Cade nodded. "Oh, yeah, that one. The guy with the cold, dead eyes. But then you already knew he was bad news."

"Hey, I didn't have anything to do with anything."

"How did you happen to have breakfast with him?"

"He sent me a text. He's a friend of a friend of mine. Had a business proposition. I met him for breakfast. That was it."

"Yet you decided not to stay for breakfast?"

"I didn't like the offer," he said bluntly. "And this is partly why." He motioned at the two of them. "Who needs this shit?"

"What kind of shit?" Cade snapped.

"Jail time shit. I've done a lot of jobs for a lot of people, but I know how to hedge my bets on which ones will land me in jail. And I didn't get the right vibes off this guy."

"What kind of vibes did you get?"

"Bad ones. My mama didn't raise no fool."

Cade nodded. "So tell us what the job was?"

But the man shut up at that point, as if realizing anything else would get him in trouble.

Laszlo smirked. "In case you think that silence will help you, you need to rethink. This guy is suspected of at least seven deaths, potentially more."

The man stared at them, his jaw opening wide. "Holy shit. I've definitely got nothing to do with any of that."

Cade waited. He wanted the man's name and some ID information and was looking for an opportunity to tackle him and take his wallet if need be. He wouldn't do it if they didn't have to. Often honey got more information than poison. However, he wasn't going to give him too much more time.

Fear warred with anger on the man's face.

Cade waited. When the stranger still didn't say anything, Cade asked, "What's your name?"

The man shrugged. "None of your business. You're the ones who broke into my room. I don't have to tell you anything."

"We already know the name you registered under with the hotel obviously," Laszlo said quietly. "But if I find out it's not your real name, then I'll be really pissed."

The man shifted his gaze to him. "So, what are you guys? The bone breakers when people say no to the boss man?"

"Not at all. We're the good guys. It's our families who are all being wiped out by the boss man's murderous acts."

The second man's eyes widened, and there was a hint of terror in them. He held up his hands and backed away. "Hey, I seriously had nothing to do with any of that."

"If that is the truth, then why are you holding off on telling us what this was all about today?"

"You know what he'll do to me if he finds out I talked to you?"

"You know what we'll do to you if you don't talk to us?" Laszlo's voice was hard. "Seven of us were blasted to hell, and one of our unit died. And since then we've been slowly losing family members."

The man's jaw worked to swallow convulsively. Then he sagged to the floor.

Cade stepped forward, one foot already on the guy's out-stretched right arm as he reached under the bed.

The guy held up his other hand, nodding toward his briefcase, visible underneath the bed. "Look. I'm just pulling out folders. I don't have a gun."

Cade wasn't sure he believed him. "Use your left hand and move slowly." He kept a close eye on the man as he pulled out his briefcase, then disengaged his foot from his other arm.

"This is all I know." He flipped open the briefcase on the bed for Cade to see and then grabbed a folder and handed it over.

Cade snatched it away, noting the man's name was War-ren Watson. He turned the folder so Laszlo could see. "Is that the name he registered under?"

Laszlo nodded. "It is."

"Hope you're not planning on staying in this business as a pro," Cade said. "I'm not sure you have the skills for it."

The man snorted. "I don't need to have the skills. I wasn't expecting to get into something like this. He wanted me to move some money. I swear that's all."

"Courier?" Cade motioned with his head toward Warren's briefcase that had a locking wrist cuff on it. "Is that what you do?"

"I do, but normally it's within the city. I don't travel across county lines."

"Good thing. It's pretty hard to hide."

"I know. But he told me that it was a special job, that I'd get well paid, and that I just needed a couple days in town. I assumed, at the time, because of the work I do, that he wanted me to courier money around town for him for two days. And, yes, that does happen in big-business deals. I've been kept in a city for five days while money exchanged hands on a continuous basis."

"Interesting job."

"And yet it comes with a hell of a lot of risk," Warren said. He pointed at the folder in Cade's hand. "If you check that out, you'll see it's just a series of emails back and forth. Take them. I don't want them."

"You have the originals on your laptop?"

Warren nodded. "I do."

"When is your flight?"

"Tomorrow," Warren said.

"Get an earlier flight."

Warren stared at him in surprise. "Why?"

"Because if we identified who you are and found you, then he can too. He's doing a hell of a job cleaning up any loose threads," Cade said in a serious tone. "For your own safety, I highly suggest you leave. Does he have any idea who you are or how to contact you?"

The man shook his head. "No, we went through a contact."

"We would like the contact's name," Laszlo said in no uncertain terms.

Warren motioned at the folder. "His email address is on them." He glanced around nervously, obviously shaken by their warning. He stopped and looked at them. "Are you serious?"

"He's either killed people himself or had all those people I mentioned earlier killed on his request. So, yes, we're damn serious."

"Shit." He grabbed his phone and started making calls.

Laszlo looked at Cade. "Do you need anything else?"

"Yeah," Laszlo turned to Warren. "A description of our bearded man. And did he say anything about the job?"

"No. I already told you. He wanted me to move money across borders. I don't do that. I'm not a smuggler. I'm a courier."

"A fine line for some people."

Warren snorted. "A fine line for a lot of people but not me. I thought it was a straight-up deal. I've always trusted my contact. So now I don't know what the hell to do."

"You might want to warn your contact too," Laszlo said. "Because this is a bad deal. All around."

On that note a hard knock came on the hotel room door. Laszlo glanced at Warren.

He stared at the door with a wide-eyed looked. In a low voice he said, "I didn't contact anyone."

The knock came again.

Laszlo and Cade slipped around the corner into the

bathroom. Cade waved at Warren. "If you want to open the door, check the peephole first."

He walked over nervously and stared through the peephole. "Hello?"

"I have a delivery for you," the man on the other side of the door said.

Warren frowned. "I didn't order anything."

"Open the door, please, sir, so I can give it to you."

Something spiked at the back of Cade's neck. That instinctive warning that said something was about to blow up in his face. He grabbed Warren and pulled him into the bathroom just as he heard gunshots, and the door exploded in front of him. Echoing outside was the sound of running footsteps.

As the man took off, Laszlo was out the door, running fast after him.

Cade looked at Warren. "Yeah, we're serious. Get the hell out of here now."

Warren nodded, his whole body shaking. "Thank you for the warning."

"You'd be in even worse shape if we found it was more than a warning you needed." Cade spoke in a hard voice. "But enough people have died. Make sure you're not the next one." And Cade took off after Laszlo.

Laszlo went left; Cade took the elevator. He hit the bottom for the lobby floor and stepped in. In no time, he was stepping out again. He walked over to the front desk. "A man just shot up guest room 804. He's taken off down the stair exit. A friend of ours is after him, but I suggest you call security and see if you can find any sign of him. Oh, and that room door will need to be fixed."

Cade took off out the front door, looking for Laszlo. He

found him standing in the parking lot, his hands on his hips, staring down the highway. Cade raced up to him. "Any sign of him?"

"He wasn't alone. He had a getaway vehicle."

"Please don't tell me it was a Lexus?"

Laszlo shook his head. "No. It wasn't. It was just a small hatchback. But they're gone."

"Did you get a chance to see the license plate?"

Laszlo shook his head. "No. For all I know, he called an Uber to wait for him."

"At least we saved one life today," Cade said quietly. "Let the police handle the rest of this one. But considering what we just went through, I don't want to leave Faith alone."

Laszlo shook his head. "No, we won't do that. Let's get her under protection right now."

CHAPTER 11

WHEN THE DOORBELL rang, she frowned as she walked toward it. "The least you could do is call and let me know you were coming," she called out.

She threw the door open. And froze. It wasn't Cade. It was a stranger with a hard look to his gaze.

"Hello," the man said, standing outside her door. "My name is Erick. I'm a friend of Cade's."

"What are you doing here?" she said, fear entering her voice. "And why should I believe you?"

He pulled up his phone and held it for her to see. She read **Erick, go to Faith's house immediately until I get there.**

She gasped. "What's happened? What's wrong?"

"We think there was an attempt on the life of the second man from the coffee house this morning," he said quietly.

She watched as he looked from one side to the other. "But I would feel better talking about this inside, not out here in the hall."

"And I'd feel a lot better if Cade had called me and told me that you were coming."

"I'm sure he did. Have you checked your phone lately?"

She frowned. She'd put her phone on Silent while she did her yoga routine. "Just a minute." She shut and locked her door, then raced to grab her phone off the living room coffee table and, sure enough, found a text from Cade. **Sending Erick to watch over you until I get there. Let him in. He's a good guy.**

She walked back to the door, as she clicked on another text to see an image come up. It was a picture of Erick. She unlocked the door and let him in. "It's a good thing Cade sent a photo ID."

"It's standard protocol when we're not sure who'll be on the other side of the door."

"Now tell me what happened," she demanded, leading the way into the living room.

He explained what he knew. "And that's the last Laszlo said. I know Cade is on his way, but it's rush hour."

"And Laszlo?"

"He's headed to the hospital to check on Badger, a friend of ours who's just had surgery. We're short on men, so Laszlo is doing a quick check to make sure everybody's okay."

"Either you need to hire more men or you need to collect everyone into one spot," she said, only half joking. "I'm tempted to grab some extra flights and work these next couple days."

"That's not a bad idea," he said quietly. He did a quick walk-through of the small apartment and frowned at the door.

As he opened his mouth, she held up her hand. "Cade already told me the security is crap."

He nodded. "It doesn't matter how good the security is. If someone is intent on getting in, they'll get in."

She sat down, her face paling. "I can't believe this is all happening."

"You were just in the wrong place at the wrong time."

"If it hadn't been for the parking lot incident today, I would have said you were all nuts," she admitted. "I saw Cade in Norway over a couple days, but that's it."

"And you had coffee with him this morning at the coffee shop?"

"Sure, and? What about it? Unless this guy has hacked Cade's phone, how would he know anything about me?"

Erick looked at her thoughtfully. "That's an interesting thought. I'm not sure what it would take for somebody who's not in the industry or in law enforcement to get a copy of them."

"You mean, copies of Cade's phone records to see that he contacted my cell phone?"

Erick nodded. "We have some information coming through and need hackers to give us a hand on that. So maybe they can check our phones as well."

"What do you mean, *information coming*?" she asked.

"I mean, the man almost killed today had a folder with copies of communications he had with a middleman who'd set up this job for him. We are hoping, if we can follow that up, we'll get somewhere."

"So you can catch the man who ran down Laszlo's father? Or is this someone who was hired to do all these murders?"

"That I can't tell you." He smiled and changed the topic. "Cade said something about Chinese?"

She snorted at his quick change of subjects. "Like I can think about food right now."

"You need to. Because at any point you might need to run."

She stopped and stared at him. "Run?" she asked in shock. "You don't mean that literally, do you?"

He shrugged. "Maybe." He thought about it, then nodded. "I definitely do. I suggest you pack a bag. Make it enough for a couple days. You shouldn't stay here. This guy knows you live in this apartment building. I'm sure Cade is considering options right now."

"I can't just pack up my life and move," she protested, but already she was standing, walking to her bedroom. "I can pack an overnight bag, but it has to be temporary. I've got to go to work in a couple days."

"Going to work is one thing. I can see why that might be what you want to do, but we'll have to take a pause and consider if that's the best thing to do."

"Are you considering I might be in danger from my coworkers?"

"Not necessarily but you are connected to a lot of people in your work. And what we don't want to do is put other people in danger because of you."

She stared at him wordlessly and entered her bedroom. There she took out her regular flight bag and packed for a few days. Her mind was almost numb, her fingers working automatically, doing something she'd done many times before. Thank heavens. Because if she required her brain to get into gear right now, nothing would get done.

When she had her bag packed, she carried it out to the living room to find Erick had a Chinese food take-out menu in his hand.

"Where did you find that?" she asked suspiciously.

Looking apologetic, he pointed to the mail she'd dropped on the coffee table. "From there."

She nodded. "Oh."

He chuckled. "Honest, I'm one of the good guys."

She rubbed her tired face. "I don't know who or what

you are, and I don't know who or what Cade is. All I know is, I went to Norway to be at my best friend's bedside and ended up in hell." She glanced at him. "Maybe you could call the hospital for me while you're here?"

Agreeably he nodded, pulled out his phone and sent a text. Then sat down and looked at the take-out menu. His phone rang moments later.

She sat down beside him and asked, "How do you know the hospital number by heart?"

"I don't. I'm talking to Laszlo. Seeing if he has an update."

The conversation was a whole lot longer than she thought it would be. But there was very little change in the inflection of Erick's voice. She didn't know if that was a good thing or a bad thing. She waited quietly until he was done; then she said, "And?"

"Her condition has been upgraded slightly, as in she's responding to stimulus, like moving her feet, moving her hand. They are hoping they can reduce the drug dosage again over the next couple days."

She threw her arms around him, hugging him tightly. "Thank you, thank you, thank you," she cried.

He hugged her back and laughed.

She sat back in the chair with her hand over her mouth. "Oh, my gosh! I'm so happy to hear that." She settled back. "Of course Mary never said anything to me."

"Do you trust Mary?"

She shrugged. "No. I can't say I do. As much as I want to, her behavior over Elizabeth's accident is very troubling. But I don't know if it's religious, simple negativity, or if she really did do something to hurt Elizabeth."

"There is a big difference between actively killing somebody and doing something to cause their death. The latter could be as simple as recognizing an opportunity," he said quietly. "As far as I understand, the hospital's been given no instructions to withhold care."

She smiled. "I have to admit it worries me. I'm afraid, if Elizabeth wakes up and goes into some kind of trauma, they won't bring her back again."

"Let's just say, from what the detective has told us, there's nothing like that in her file. Doesn't mean Mary can't change it, but, with Elizabeth's steady progress, the doctors would get suspicious."

"Right, and, of course, Mary is very private and doesn't like any kind of intrusions."

"That also doesn't mean she wants her sister to live. Sending you away was within her rights, but it's up to the doctors to keep Elizabeth alive the best they can."

She nodded. "Right."

Just then there was a knock on the door. Erick bolted to his feet and motioned for her to go to the bedroom. He walked to the front door and chuckled, calling out, "Faith, it's Cade." He opened the door, and Cade walked in, his arms full.

"I guess that's why you didn't text to say you were coming up?" Erick asked as he took the bags from him and headed to the kitchen.

Cade walked around the living room, took one look at Faith and smiled. "There you are."

She raced into his arms, and he closed them around her gently.

"Honest, we'll keep you safe."

She squeezed him even tighter, then whispered, "Thank you."

He gently disengaged himself. "Thank you for what? For sending Erick over or for bringing the Chinese food?"

She chuckled, took one look at the size of the bags, and her jaw dropped. "Are you serious? How many are we feeding?"

He gave her an injured look. "Well, Erick and I need to eat, unless you were planning on eating it all."

She snorted, heading to the kitchen, Cade behind her. "I can't begin to eat all this."

"We never know. We might end up with company."

She narrowed her gaze. "Who would that be?"

"Not necessarily anybody, but Talon is on his way back."

"You heard from him?" Erick asked.

Cade nodded. "He called you but got voice mail. He left a message for me, saying he was coming back."

"Any idea why?"

Cade nodded. "The tracker ended up at a truck stop. That's when Talon realized it had been switched to a truck with an old lady driving."

Erick whispered, "Shit. Of course it was."

"How long 'til he gets in?"

"Probably another forty-five minutes."

"Yeah, so he'll definitely want food."

"Not sure he'll come here though."

Feeling better, and knowing Cade was safe too, Faith wondered if that wasn't partly the reason behind her reaction earlier. She got up and put on a new pot of coffee. She didn't need any caffeine, as she was jittery enough, but she figured the men would like it.

When she turned around with plates in her hand, she found the men pulling out at least a half-dozen Chinese dishes from the to-go bags Cade had brought in. Something about smelling the aroma filling the kitchen woke up her hunger. "Five minutes ago I was sure I wouldn't be able to eat. But now I smell all this and, like, … wow."

Cade nodded. "And you need to eat if you can."

She winced. "Yes, Erick mentioned something about it earlier."

"Did he tell you to pack a bag?"

She nodded. "Yes, he did."

"Good. We might stay here for the night. I'm not sure. We'll wait and see what Talon has to say when he gets in."

"I suppose he already knows where I live too?"

"Oh, yeah. By now all of our team does."

She sighed. "As long as I won't end up on some FBI Watch List, where I won't be allowed into any of the countries I travel to," she warned, "because that can't happen. Then you're putting my career in jeopardy too."

The men both shook their heads, and Cade said, "No, nothing like that will happen."

With all the dishes open in front of her, she served herself a healthy portion and sat down to eat at her tiny kitchen table. "This isn't from my usual place." She grabbed the receipt, stunned at the amount of money Cade had spent on it. "But I have to admit, it's really tasty."

"It's one of my favorites," Cade said. "I was driving past it anyway. So that's what I decided on."

She nodded and smiled. She was halfway done with her plate, when the men were already heading for seconds. She glanced at the food. "Do I need to put some away for Talon?" she joked.

Just then Cade's phone buzzed. "It's Talon. He's heading to his place. Too pissed and tired to come here. He says, if we need him, call him."

Erick nodded. "In that case I'll have more. Just give me a minute or two to finish what I've got."

She stared at the amount of food still on his plate. "Are you serious?"

He chuckled. "We'd never leave him short. But we're hungry. There's nothing like a little gunfight to bring on the appetite."

"Did you guys fire back at him?" Her face showed horror. "Did anybody get hurt?"

Both men shook their heads. "No, but the gunman got away, and Warren Watson, who was the second man at the coffee shop this morning, changed flights to go home as soon as he can."

"Will he be safe at home?" she asked.

The men looked at each other and back at her, shrugging. "No way to know. When you get involved with men like this Lexus guy, there's just no easy answer, and there's no easy out."

"So how much was the second guy involved in this?"

"He wasn't. He made the trip, thinking he would be a courier. Instead his contact wanted him to be a smuggler."

"It's hard to even imagine this stuff happens."

"I know, but it does, all the time." Cade shuffled the folder he'd brought in with the Chinese food and opened it up on the kitchen table.

Erick grabbed his full plate and moved to where he could take a look at the folder. He read through the emails while Cade topped up his plate.

Faith glanced at Cade. "Anything interesting?"

"Some interesting emails we'll get some people to check on. Other than that, it's as Warren said."

"And the contact?" Erick asked.

"Oh, it's a real person, and it looks like a viable email, but, of course, it'll be rerouted through a bunch of servers, so we aren't likely to get very much from it."

"I think we should contact him," Erick said, "see if he will help us track down the man who tried to kill Warren. Apparently he's worked with Warren for a long time. So maybe he'd do it as a friend."

"We might need Warren for that," Cade suggested.

"I plan on contacting him as soon as we finish eating," Erick said. "And, by the way, Badger is awake."

Faith looked from one to the other and saw the relief and love in Cade's face at the mention of his friend. "I gather that's good news?"

Cade smiled at her. "About as good as if Elizabeth woke up right now and wanted to know where you were."

She smiled inside. "And that would be the best news ever," she said. "I'm really happy for your friend." Then she added almost as an afterthought, "And for you too."

He nodded. "Is he allowed visitors yet?" Cade asked Erick.

"Kat said she'd let us know. At the moment, no. But, once the doctors upgrade his condition and check him over, it should be fine."

"Thank heavens for that," Cade said. "You know the first thing he'll ask about is what progress we've made."

Erick chuckled. "Outside of the fact he said something very personal to Kat, the next thing out of his mouth was asking for an update. Kat told him that she would get one for him and would tell him the next time he woke up."

"And, of course, that would be the next phone call we make."

Faith realized how lucky they were. She had Elizabeth. But they had not only each other, they had five more men in the same group. "You're truly blessed to have all of you."

The men looked at each other and nodded. "We know."

CADE SAT BACK with a happy full tummy and said, "That was good."

"It was. Thank you for picking it up. Now what will you do?"

He glanced over at Erick to see him staring back at them with a slightly raised eyebrow. .

In a tone of frustration, she said, "And stop discussing it between the two of you. I'd like to know how this pertains to me and what I'm supposed to do."

"We weren't discussing anything. He was asking me what we'll do too," Cade said smoothly. "Not necessarily sure I've an answer, except for the fact we'll continue to pursue all leads, make sure you're never alone. Because we can't take a chance of this guy coming back after you."

"But there's no reason for him to come after me," she said quietly. "And, as far as somebody always staying with me, you do remember I'm a pilot, right? I can fly all over the world for free and hide away until this is over."

"And when do you think it'll be over? Do you really want to take the chance of coming home too soon, or, even worse, him being able to track you through your airline, finding out where you are, catching you unaware where you have no protection?" Cade spoke quietly. He reached over and covered her hand with his. "I'm not trying to be difficult or to scare you unnecessarily, but you have to realize that, right now, you're in an ugly scenario, and solutions are not exactly fast coming."

She slumped in her chair. "So, what you're saying is, I'm stuck not being able to live my life until you capture this guy? And he's been out killing friends and family of yours for two years without you knowing?" Her voice rose an octave at the end.

"That's not fair," Erick said. "We only realized what might be happening a couple weeks or so ago. How does anybody connect accidents in different parts of the world and think that any one person could be responsible?"

She had the grace to look ashamed. "I'm sorry. It's just, hearing you guys talk about something that's been going on for so long, it's like a life sentence you've handed down to me."

"Not us," Cade reminded her. "We aren't doing this to you. We're protecting you from this man."

"Do you think the same man, the one you've been targeting, is an international serial killer? If all these accidents or deaths are spread worldwide, maybe he hired several people?"

"It's quite possible he did, or maybe he did the first couple *accidents* and then decided it would be too hot for him to continue doing this, and so he hired a couple other people. There are really no answers yet."

"What's the chance it's all just in your imagination?" Her gaze went from one to the other.

"Again, that's possible, but not likely." Cade frowned at the expression on her face. "Faith, I will do everything I can to be there for you." When she remained silent, he added, "That includes my team and two other teams we can rely on as well. Trust me. Trust us," Cade said, nodding Erick's way. "We will get this guy. We are personally invested in finding him. Unfortunately you've been added to his radar. We are all working on this and hoping for a fast resolution, but it won't come fast enough for us. Or for you. Not yet. Hang in there."

Frustrated, she put the lids on the empty containers, stacking them in the bag the food came in. "What does it mean when you say, I can't be alone?"

"It means, I'm either staying here with you or you'll be staying at my house," Cade said.

She shook her head. "It's too unbelievable. This happens on TV shows, in books. Not in my life." Her movements were short and angry, as she rolled down the top of the paper bag with all the garbage inside and got up to pour herself a cup of coffee.

Just then Erick's phone rang. Erick looked over at Cade as he pulled it out. "It's Levi." Erick stood and walked to the living room to hear the call better.

Cade waited, but he couldn't hear enough to be of interest.

Faith sat down beside him. "I could go back to Norway."

"Would that help you any? Would it help Elizabeth? You are still barred from visiting your friend. Unless she wakes up and can override her sister's orders."

Faith frowned and started to play with the spoon on the table. "She should be waking up soon though."

"Maybe, but until she's awake and has a say in her own care, you know you're not allowed there."

"It's so damn frustrating," she muttered. She leaned back in her chair and closed her eyes.

"But, in a way, it's a good thing. Because you could be tracked there by our target. He knows where you live. It's just a matter of following you." He studied her face, the delicate cheekbones, the curve of her lips, seeing the pallor and the fatigue of the last few days. "I'm so sorry you ended up in the middle of this. I would do anything to stop you from being in danger."

"I don't blame you. But I wish there was a way out of this hell."

"Now that we've mobilized a lot of men—former and current SEALs—to give us a hand, we'll get somewhere. Levi is just one of many. Having a larger team will make a big difference in finding whether these deaths in the last couple years are all connected."

She studied him for a long moment, then asked timidly, "Like your sister?"

Instantly his stomach clenched, and his heart seized. He could feel his jawline stiffening. But he nodded. "Like my sister. We lost our parents when we were young and were raised by our aunt and uncle. There was just the two of us. She died seventeen months ago in a multicar pileup."

She stared at him in horror. "But you think it was this guy?"

"I have to consider it."

"Couldn't it have been an accident? Something he would have appreciated because it would maximize your pain, but maybe he didn't do anything to cause it?"

"It's quite possible. Again we don't know. We can only surmise."

"How many other people recently died in your family?"

"Just my sister."

She winced. After a moment she said, "Did you see the accident report?"

"Not at the time. But Erick has been collecting the reports from all the various incidences for us to take a closer look at. I just didn't want to examine that one too closely."

That's when he realized she'd turned her hand inside his, and now she held his gently, her thumb moving along the index finger, offering comfort as she could. He sighed. "Any death is difficult. But when it's your last close family member, it's really hard."

"Your aunt and uncle?"

He gave her a lopsided grin. "They did their duty, but that's about it."

"If you suspect something awful did happen to her, sometimes reading the report makes it easier. Like, you could read how it was just bad road conditions, and it was truly an accident."

He shook his head. "I can't. Not that. I'm counting on the rest of my team to figure that out and to let me know. But if somebody did deliberately run her off the road or ran her car into somebody else's, that would be very difficult for me to read, to envision, to relive," he said quietly. "But my situation is no different than the other guys'."

"Either way, it's difficult for everyone," she said. "And, for that, I'm sorry."

Erick walked back over to join them. "Levi and Tesla are taking a look at the accident reports themselves. He wanted clarification on a couple of them. But he particularly looked at yours, Cade."

Feeling his jaw seize a little bit more, hating to even ask the question but knowing he had to hear the answer, he asked, "What did he find?"

"She was involved in a multivehicle accident. But they're not so sure her injuries were caused by that accident."

Fear stuck in his throat. "What do you mean?"

"According to Levi, a head injury is what caused her death, but you know that."

Cade nodded. "Yes. She wasn't wearing a seat belt and hit the windshield." He felt Faith's fingers squeeze around his, holding him firmly in place. Cade took a deep breath and asked, "Why?"

"Because the accident report said the speed she was going didn't justify the force that caused her head injury."

For a long moment he didn't understand. He stared at Erick and shook his head. "I don't get it."

"The traffic report stated she had spun out of control, possibly hitting her head on the windshield. But Levi says there's a good chance that someone hit her over the head hard enough to kill her and then made it look like it was the car accident. Leaving her inside the car, her stationary vehicle could have caused the multicar pileup."

"So somebody came to her car, in the middle of a winter blizzard, opened the vehicle door, struck her with something across her head at the front temple where she would have hit the windshield, possibly cracked the windshield at the same time, and nobody saw it happen?"

"You said yourself there was a whiteout," Erick said. "Levi has looked at all the documents relating to this incident, and she was going less than twenty miles an hour on the highway."

"She wasn't slammed into from behind? That would have sent her flying forward."

"Not according to the accident reports. There was only minor damage to her vehicle."

"But they said it was a multicar pileup," Cade exclaimed.

"As in several vehicles were in an accident. Yes. However, each accident report said several other vehicles smashed together to avoid her car, as she was stopped crosswise on the highway itself."

Cade stared at him. "So what you're saying is," he said in a harsh voice, "my sister was murdered."

CHAPTER 12

FAITH DIDN'T KNOW what to say. Poor Cade. He looked so devastated. It was just too unbelievable to even consider somebody would have gone to the trouble to take out so many family members, all related to his SEAL unit. There was so much hate in the world, and she didn't understand any of it.

"I'm so sorry." She stared down at her knuckles. They should be screaming in pain from the grip he had on her fingers, but he didn't even notice how tightly he held her hand. Caught in his own cloud of pain and agony, he had grabbed on to anything that would help him stay in control. With her other hand, she gently stroked the back of his. "Levi is sure, is he?" she asked Erick. "I don't know him myself."

"Excellent military man. Ice, his partner, is equal to him in so many ways, and her father is a well-respected doctor. So her father took a look at the injuries detailed in the reports as well. They reconstructed the accident according to the reports, and don't forget, several other reports were made about this same incident from the drivers of the other vehicles involved. Cade's sister's vehicle was the one that caused the crash because the others were trying to avoid hitting her.

"There was no sign of another vehicle prior to the

pileup. They assumed she had slammed her head into the windshield because of her lack of a seat belt. And sometimes it happens that way. You can get a bleed on the brain and die. In her case, the initial head injury was enough to kill her instantly. But it wasn't likely caused by the windshield."

Faith stared at Cade, still so silent that it worried her. "But, if the windshield was damaged, there is no real way to know for sure, is there?" Faith asked.

"They have the various police reports, the photos from the scenes and the EMTs evaluation of Cade's sister at the scene," Erick said. "Remember? And they reconstructed the head injury. It's a different angle than the blow on the windshield. The traumatic head injury was on the left side. The blow to the windshield was on the right side."

"And, of course, she wasn't traveling very fast," Faith said quietly. "And with no blow from behind to send her forcefully forward, then it certainly brings up the question of how?"

"Exactly," Erick said.

"Will the police reopen the investigation?" Faith asked, Cade still so quiet.

He shook his head. "No. And honestly that's not what we're trying to do. Cade's sister has been dead and buried for almost a year and a half already. The problem is, finding out who did this."

"I don't suppose there are photographs of the other vehicles or the tire tracks?"

Erick's gaze lit up with interest. "That's a really good question. I do have the entire file, and, as far as I can see, there were photos of the other vehicles and of her vehicle but nothing of the tracks themselves. But don't forget. By the time anybody came to her aid, there were already multiple emergency vehicles involved and multiple footprints from the EMTs and the police. Not to mention the falling snow."

"Of course. And, if the evidence wasn't preserved, there's no way to go back." She sighed, glancing over at Cade. The grip on her fingers had slowly eased, but he was lost in his own misery. She motioned toward him, then said to Erick, "What about the other accidents involving your team?"

Erick sat down at the table. "I don't have any of the accident reports with me," he admitted. "Levi and Mason have very large teams—Levi is former military, and Mason is active military—but, in both groups, they have very skilled people working with them."

"So you trust their findings?"

Erick nodded once, saying, "Absolutely."

"And how do you tie all these accidents together?"

"The only tie I can see is the fact they're all related to our unit."

She settled back. "That's a big tie."

"It's a *really* big tie. I can't think of any other justifiable reason for so many accidents. It doesn't make any sense."

She had to give him that. "And you guys can't think of any single one person who hates you so much?"

He shook his head. "No. And that's another problem because that's a lot for somebody to hate."

"What about from your military service?" she asked.

"We've all gone through various missions in our heads, but we haven't been able to come up with anything."

"So you're all connecting these more recent serial killings back to the land mine accident that took the seven of you out, or eight of you, considering the one who died?" she hurriedly corrected. "Because that's a leap in itself."

"The leap isn't so much from the original accident to

these. If we acknowledge that the original land mine explosion was a setup, and our team was deliberately targeted, then we have to follow through with the understanding that the subsequent accidents weren't accidents either. They were just as targeted."

She sat in silence, contemplating the scope of one man's devastating actions. Then she realized something else. She thought about it for a long moment, then said, "I don't think the man you're chasing in Santa Fe is the same man responsible for all these accidents. I mean, he's definitely connected. Maybe he did cause the accidents or murdered these people," she said slowly, thinking it through. "But you have to consider he was moving money. That's why he wanted the courier. So I think he's been paid to do them. At least paid to do a lot of them if not all of them."

She felt Cade's start of surprise. Slowly he looked at her, and she watched as realization came into his gaze.

He turned to stare at Erick. "She's right." His voice was harsh, as if unused, rusty, and laden with emotion. "There has to be a reason why he was moving large amounts of money."

"That's likely to hide the source." Erick leaned forward with excitement. "So that leads to the next question – why would he want to move the money?"

"Because he can't spend it here," she said. "Or because it's getting too hot for him to stay here, and he wants to go somewhere else. But that means moving his money with him, to wherever he's headed."

The three of them looked at each other, and Erick brought out his phone. "We need to find out any known associates of this guy. See if we can track down whoever is behind it." He glanced at Cade. "Does that make sense to you?"

Cade shook his head, as if coming from a long way away, then cleared his throat to focus on the topic at hand. "It makes more sense than if it's all the same person. It's risky to orchestrate all these supposed accidents and not get caught. Although, with as much time as there was between incidences, he had time to plan meticulously."

"This Santa Fe guy did the Norway accident with Laszlo's father. We know that," she said. "Because that's how you tracked him back to Santa Fe. If any had been done here, you wouldn't doubt it being him as well. What you need to do is place him at the other accidents, if possible, see if he has any associates here in New Mexico who might be paying him for these jobs."

"If he's getting paid in cash, that person has to be local. Even if it's a middleman, that individual will lead us to the boss man at the top. If it's bank transfers or offshore accounts, it'll have a digital footprint," Erick said. "But Levi has Sienna, and she does a lot of forensic accounting. Maybe they can track his bank accounts and see."

"And if it's cash?" Faith asked.

"It's much harder these days to deposit or cash out large sums," Erick explained. "So, most of these hired-gun guys, if they have cash, they keep it as cash. But then it gets much harder to move from place to place too. It's not impossible, but it's definitely harder."

"So chances are," Faith continued, "he's been paid in a large sum for these jobs, and he wants to take it away with him and is now having trouble moving the money. Maybe he doesn't know how. Maybe he doesn't have the job skills for that. Or maybe he was counting on it not being a problem, and he's come up to this unexpected snag. It's easy to travel the world alone," Faith said. "I know. I do it for a living. But it's an entirely different case if this guy is leaving a paper trail by transferring the money from bank account to bank account, like I do sometimes."

"And those we can track," Cade said quietly. "I think that's the avenue we need to look at."

"We have the name on the driver's license," Erick stated. "And we have the car registration, which is in the same name, so Levi is working on tracking down any information on that."

"We need to contact the go between and Warren Watson," Cade said.

Erick nodded. "I've sent in a couple email requests to the middleman and a request to Warren Watson. So far I haven't heard back from either."

"And no luck tracking down the middleman's email address?"

"No. It's a proxy server, which was expected. But I suspect he's getting the messages. He just doesn't want to get involved."

At that, Faith decided she needed to shut down for the night. She got up. "It's late. I need some rest."

Cade nodded. "I'll stay here for the night. Are you okay if the two of us sit here and talk for a bit before Erick leaves?"

She nodded. "That's fine. Just make sure you lock up after him." Her tone was dry because, of course, he would do that without her reminder. She headed into her bedroom.

Cade said, "A little too much?"

She heard Cade's comment as she shut the door. She wanted to shout and scream, *Of course it's too much.* She was a normal average human being. She had worked hard to get to be where she was and was already dealing with Elizabeth's accident and Mary's odd standpoint. But to think somebody was out there systematically picking off these men's family members—after blowing them up in a military truck, serving their country—that was just too much.

What they had to do was find the man behind it all. She now suspected, as they already did, that was who had arranged the original accident. But to think that much hate lived in this world was just beyond her. It wasn't how she wanted to live her life. And yet she was obviously embroiled, and no amount of self-pity would take her out of it.

ERICK LEFT SOON after Faith went to bed. He promised to check in with Cade in the morning.

With Faith in bed, the apartment now felt empty and was too quiet. Cade washed the few coffee cups and set them upside down on a tea towel on the counter. It wasn't worth turning on the dishwasher for so few dishes. He did the same with the few plates and forks they had used with dinner. Then he turned to look at the couch. She hadn't been exactly helpful in setting up a place for him for the night, but he was a big boy. It was warm in the apartment; he walked to the glass French doors, opened them wide and let the cool air flow through the room.

Inside he was still traumatized by the news that his sister had likely been killed while sitting in her vehicle, stunned from the initial car accident. But those car-related injuries she should have survived. He'd wondered at the time, but he dared not ask too many questions. It had been devastating to know she had died as it was. Getting the details would have been just too much. All he wanted to know was that she hadn't suffered. And, according to the detective at the time, she hadn't.

Now he realized, while she had not suffered, she hadn't been given a chance to live. He lay down on the couch, his shoes at the front door, and propped his legs up on the arm at the other end. He didn't know what size couches came in these days, but it seemed like everybody had little ones. What happened to something that would fit big guys like him?

As he lay here, Laszlo texted him. **Is all okay?**

It's all okay, he replied. **Except for the fact Levi and Ice's dad have determined my sister was struck over the head after her accident, and that was what killed her.** As soon as he sent that, his phone rang.

"What the hell?" Laszlo snapped. "Do you think they are correct?"

"According to what Levi told Erick, the evidence was pretty foolproof. The head injury was on the left side, but the crack in the windshield came from her right side. It's as if the killer had something in his hand, swung it in an arc, and it came around on the right."

"Like a baseball bat. Your sister's lying against the driver's side window. He hits her, coming around with as much force as he can, and she hits the windshield?" Laszlo asked. "And then what? Propped up your sister again?" His voice was raised in outrage. "Jesus, I can't think of one single person in our world who would do something like that."

"Neither can I," Cade said in a tired voice. Just hearing Laszlo discuss his sister's final moments was enough to hurt. "Chances are, whoever it was probably caused her accident in the first place. All the other vehicles in the multicar pileup apparently happened because her vehicle was in the way.

They all tried to avoid her, to hit their brakes. The road was in bad shape with the ongoing blizzard. So one spun out, hit another, hit another, hit another. That type of thing."

"I thought that's what happened originally, and your sister was just in the middle of it all."

"Apparently she was the first vehicle, and there would have been a lot of tire tracks to help recreate the accident, but it was snowing heavily. So, within seconds, Mother Nature had completely wiped out any evidence there was to find."

"In other words, there's no way to prove what Levi says is true. Since we don't know who the attacker is, there's no point getting the police to reopen the case."

"According to them, it's a done deal."

"There was no autopsy done on your sister, was there?"

"No," he said quietly. "There was no need."

"No, of course not. Plus you were in between surgeries, trying to stand on your own two feet. Like the rest of us, the last two years have been a struggle to just survive. Dealing with the personal losses on top of that has just crushed all of us to the ground."

"Which is exactly what this asshole is trying to do."

"Do you ever wonder when he'll stop?"

"I was just considering that," Cade said quietly. "Think about it. Seven of us, Mouse, and eight of our family members. In Talon's case, his best friend. All have been taken out—or close to it, in your father's case."

"So he's injured all of us two years ago, killing Mouse. Then he's injured our friends or family afterward. Now what does he try for? Another friend or family member or does he come back around and try to take us out again?"

"I wish he would try to take us out." Cade barely held

back his anger. "That at least would give us a target. And we'd be able to see who is doing this."

"I know. It could be the only way we ever find out who is behind it." Laszlo's voice was tired. "I just heard from my brother. My father is going back into the hospital tonight."

"Why?"

"He's losing feeling in his legs," Laszlo said sadly. "Apparently it started when I was there, but he didn't want to say anything. And now it's so bad that he's tripping and falling because he can't move his legs properly."

"Is this from the accident?"

"When you're seventy-four, I'm not sure they can say yes or no, but the accident didn't help." Laszlo's voice was despondent.

Cade hated to hear that news. "Damn. It's not fair to have targeted somebody of that age. He only had a few good years left."

"I know. But, considering my brother is already dying from cancer, he probably figured that would double the torment for me."

"Who? Who could do this?" Cade snapped in rage. "I just don't get it. I've gone through with a paper and pen, listing all the missions for the five years we were in the same unit while active in the navy, including the final year we shared with Mouse. I've gone over the staff members we worked with and the support staff we worked with, our unit members, and I know we shouldn't have to question those peoples loyalties, but at least they'd have the skills to handle this. I keep coming up blank."

"I've done the same thing," Laszlo finally said. "And I've also come up with nothing. There were a couple asshole guys I didn't get along with, but they weren't anybody I had a problem with. They were just arrogant. But that goes along with the type of work we do. We all know a lot of guys in our units are arrogant asses in many ways. We must have a certain amount of self-confidence, a certain amount of bravado, to do what we do. And, every once in a while, there's someone who ticks you off."

"Except for Mouse. He never really had a chance to get that deep in," Cade said quietly. "And, for that, I'm very sorry. He was a young kid. Younger than all of us. He shouldn't have had to die so young."

"None of it should have happened. We're not to blame for what happened to Mouse. We're not to blame for what happened to any of us. Some other asshole orchestrated this whole mess. That we're still dealing with the fallout is unbelievable. But to think that the same person is going around, targeting our family members, puts this on a whole new level, and I just can't get my mind wrapped around it," Laszlo snapped.

"I hear you there. And what really bothers me is not one of us can come up with a person who would have done this."

"What if it wasn't one person?" Laszlo said, as if thinking out loud. "What if it was one of the groups we've dealt with who targeted us all, and now they've decided that, since we're still alive, they'll go after our families?"

"What? Like an Iraqi terrorist group?" Cade asked. "Why would they care? It's not just us after them. It's all the US Navy and military."

"I know. I'm just thinking out loud."

"Faith did suggest the bearded guy we've been chasing could be a hired gun. The fact that he wanted to hire Warren to move money adds credence to that. Maybe he was hired to run down your father in Norway, but he used Santa Fe as a base and was moving some of the money out of here."

"The only reason to move large amounts of cash is if that's the only way he could get paid." Laszlo quietly contemplated. "And he can still move small amounts. But, as we know, it's much harder to move bigger amounts without it being tracked."

"Lots of people still move money by the suitcase though."

"But Warren didn't want to do that. So our guy's still looking for somebody."

"What about setting a trap?" Cade said suddenly. He sat up and leaned into the arm of the couch. "What if the contact sets us up as a courier?"

"That might work," Laszlo said. "But it can't be one of us. Because, if it happens to be the same guy who's been targeting us, you know he'll recognize us."

"So, it has to be somebody else, like one of Levi's men then. But I'd sure as hell like to be the bait."

"We can't take the chance."

"No, and we need someone to set this up. It would be good to get somebody who's got a lot of international travel connections."

"Maybe Erick knows somebody we can use."

"He'll say one of Levi's men. You know that," Cade said. "And maybe that's not a bad idea. They have a lot of experience. They're also capable of dealing with assholes."

"We can make it safe—or as safe as possible," Laszlo said. "Once the money is handed over, we can pick up our bearded hired gunman and maybe even the contact person for a little chat."

"And the money. I really like the idea of hitting this hired gun by taking his money," Cade said, a snarl to his voice. "I'd like to do serious damage to him in more ways than one, but, at least if we take his money, that will help hamstring some of his operation."

"Still, don't forget. He could be just a hired gun. One of many even."

"Sure, but we take out one, and that's a connection to the next level. Eventually we've got to find the guy at the top."

"Call Erick," Laszlo said. "I have to phone the hospital and talk to my brother."

The two men hung up, and Cade called Erick.

Erick's voice was thoughtful. "It's not a bad idea. Depends if Warren will help us set it up."

"He should. It might also get the guy off his back."

"He has to answer us first though," Erick said drily. "So far he's avoiding us."

"He's probably traveling."

"Maybe. Look after Faith tonight. I'll send out a couple emails to see if I can get anybody to bite."

"We also have to find the right courier," Cade said. "It's got to be somebody who can handle this. But not somebody this guy could recognize, which means it can't be one of us."

"Meaning, it could be the same asshole who arranged our original land mine explosion, and he might recognize us?"

"Exactly."

"I'll talk to Levi."

Cade hung up, lay back down on the couch and, for the first time in several days, he felt like, maybe, just maybe, they'd get some answers. He closed his eyes and fell asleep.

CHAPTER 13

FAITH WOKE UP to darkness in her room. She lay still for a moment, her mind frozen, wondering why she'd woken up. There were noises outside, a party, some drunken reverie, but she didn't hear anything else. Until an odd noise came from the living room. She gasped and then remembered Cade was staying with her.

She threw back her covers and stood. She grabbed her robe, walked to the bedroom window, moving the curtains slightly. The moon was high. She checked the clock on the nightstand. It was just after one. She opened her bedroom door and stepped into the living room.

A quiet voice asked, "Can't sleep?"

She walked to the couch. "You're still here?"

He reached up a hand, grabbed hers and tugged her down until she was sitting in his lap.

She smiled. "I wasn't sure if you meant that. I'm sorry I left so abruptly earlier tonight. It got to be too much."

His hand moved soothingly up and down her arm. "It was getting too much for all of us," he said quietly. "I wasn't in very good shape after I heard the news about my sister either."

She sighed. "I can't imagine the level of ugly that's touching our lives right now."

Just then the noise outside increased for a few loud

screeches and yells of joy.

She chuckled. "At least somebody is having fun."

"This is what makes the world go round."

She looked around the living room. "I didn't even think to give you a blanket and pillow. Do you want anything?"

"I want you." He chuckled. "But you're not ready for that."

She glanced down at him. "I guess we've had what amounted to three meetings."

"We've had more than three meetings and at least two of them could be classified as dates." He chuckled again. "Breakfast and then Chinese tonight."

She smiled. "The thing is, I don't do short-term relationships," she said. "I found I care too deeply, and, when people move on because they don't care enough in the first place, I get hurt."

"That's good to know. Because I wasn't looking for a short-term relationship."

"Honestly you weren't looking for a relationship at all," she joked, keeping the atmosphere light. She wanted him too but wasn't sure she should take that step. And how real were the feelings coursing through her? That he was sexy and magnetic and caring were all good things, but this was a very strange set of circumstances, and she wasn't sure that being thrown together during a crisis was a good way to start a relationship. What if this sizzle between them was just fueled by the adrenaline of this drama? What if the dull and boring parts of life weren't enough to keep them together?

"Maybe we did fall into it. Or maybe the events have accelerated the normal path to a relationship," he said. "I gave up working out the vagaries of life a long time ago. I'm perfectly happy to just go with the flow in this situation."

"And what about all the craziness going on around us?"

He raised an eyebrow.

It was hard to see his face in the shadows. She realized he'd opened the double French doors, and a cool breeze wafted in. She glanced outside. The noise had calmed down, and now the moonlight shone inside. "I'm never out here at this time. It's beautiful."

"It is indeed."

His voice was thick, gentle. But there was an air of waiting to him. A stillness. And she understood what he was asking. The fact he was asking was nice, but she hated that she needed to make a decision. She would rather just have passion take them over. It was never like that. There was all this preamble that had to happen first.

She sighed and stretched out across his chest, her head on his shoulder, her nose against his chin. "Going with the flow is one thing," she said. "But in the morning the flow comes to an end."

A rumble moved up his chest and his throat. He chuckled, his voice warm and hot against her face. "True enough. But that same flow can happen again and again. Daylight might change what we have to get done. It doesn't necessarily have to affect the base of the foundation we're building."

"I'll bet you say that to all the girls," she teased.

"I haven't had a relationship since before my accident." He reached out his ungloved left hand and wrapped it around her back, and she felt the metal through her bathrobe.

"Does it make you self-conscious?"

He nodded. "Of course. There is nothing pretty about my body."

"A lot of scars, huh?"

"A lot of scars. A lot of injuries. A lot of surgeries. A lot of recovery. And, of course, there's a missing lower leg and foot and a missing arm."

She sat up slowly, turned on the light on the end table and said, "I want to see."

He looked at her in surprise, but he sat up obediently.

She helped him out of his shirt and was amazed to see the prosthetic where it met skin.

Then he removed it to show her what was left of his arm.

She reached out to touch the stump. And then looked at him, as if asking permission.

He nodded. "I'm not breakable," he joked.

She smiled and touched the end of his arm. "Does that hurt?"

"No. By now it's fairly stabilized. There's a built-in padding for cushion and support in the prosthetic." He pointed to it on the back of the couch.

"You use the arm really well."

"I do. But it took a long time to get to this point." At that, he put on his prosthetic hand once more.

She glanced down at his artificial foot.

He pulled up his pant leg, so she could see where the prosthetic leg and foot came off. But his jeans were not cooperating. He shrugged. "Sorry. If you want to see the rest, you'll have to take off a piece of clothing too."

That surprised a laugh out of her. She dropped her bathrobe and tossed it over the back of the couch.

He chuckled, shifting her off his lap and onto the couch, so he could stand. Unbuckling his jeans, he dropped his pants. There, standing in front of her in gray boxers, he kicked the jeans off to the side. And then he sat back down again, stretching out both legs.

She could see the cuff where his stump went into the artificial leg. It was a different kind of attachment than what she had seen on his arm. She ran her fingers over the top. "Doesn't it get sore when you're on your leg all the time?"

"No, but that's one of the reasons why Badger is in the hospital. He was having a lot of trouble with his. I've been lucky." He reached down, popped the button on the prosthetic and then released the gel sock that was at the bottom of his leg, showing it to her.

She bent down to study the end, her fingers gently stroking. "To think of the damage done to your body ..." She shook her head. "I can't imagine what you went through initially. But even after that, all that you must've gone through to get to this point today."

"It doesn't matter what I went through now because I've recovered. But, like I said, I'm not very pretty."

She sat back into the couch and studied his chest as he put the prosthetic leg back on.

He glanced down and winced. "Yeah, my chest is another good example. My back is too." He shifted on the couch so she could see his back.

At the touch of her finger stroking it, he winced.

Immediately she froze.

"No, don't do that. It feels great."

Again she stroked his battle-roughened skin. Normally there were hills and valleys in a perfectly healthy male form, but, in his case, there were dents where muscle should be, and scars crisscrossed his back.

When she got to his hips, he pointed out a particularly pitted place. "There was a big chunk of metal in my back there."

She gasped. "You're very lucky. I imagine you would have been paralyzed if it was over even a little bit."

"I know," he said. "And I do remind myself that I *am* very lucky."

She swept her hand down his back and around to his front, easing over some of the heavy pink scar tissue. "Will these fade?"

"With time. With more time."

She glanced at his thighs, what she could see below his boxers, and traced a finger across one particularly nasty scar that went through his knee and back down again. "That looks very painful."

"That one wasn't painful though. And it was my good leg, which is a good thing because I abused that leg trying to get the other one working."

She nodded and stroked her hand up his thigh until it rested at the lower edge of his boxers.

He shook his head. "Now you're living dangerously."

She chuckled. "Am I?" She could see his erection through the thin soft cotton. She knew, in her mind, what she was doing was a risk—aren't all relationships?—but she couldn't seem to resist. And, even knowing it would take her down a road where she may not be able to get off, she still couldn't stop herself from sliding her fingers across his thigh and up over his shaft.

He gasped, his hips coming up off the couch, as if pressing deeper into her hand.

She closed her fingers around him and whispered, "At least you didn't hurt this part of your body."

He groaned. "Hell no. That's always worked just fine."

She smiled, leaned forward, her lips just a hair away from his and said, "Prove it."

Instantly she was crushed against his chest as his lips claimed hers with the fierce kiss of both passion and possession. A heavy rush of heat flew through her, stunning her with both the speed and the potency of it. She moaned against his lips.

He released her.

She shook her head. "No, don't let me go. And definitely don't stop."

He searched her gaze for a long moment, then crushed her to him again. Just before his lips claimed hers once more, he said, "No problem. I won't let you go all night."

Overwhelmed by the unexpected emotions cascading through her, Faith found herself caught up in a storm. She was incapable of doing anything but reacting. Her body shifted and twisted in response to his every hand stroke, to every touch of his lips, to every kiss as he trailed his lips down, then across her chest, stopping at the tip of her breast to softly suckle it with his mouth. She moaned and arched, her hands reaching up to grasp and hold him close.

She didn't know how to respond to these crazy emotions. She hadn't expected to feel anything like this. She shuddered as he lifted his head and blew gently on the wet tip of her breast, her body clenching in desire. He moved over to her other breast, giving it just as much attention. But she wanted his mouth on hers. She wanted more of those drug-inducing kisses.

She lifted his head, but he wasn't having any of it. His hands stroked down her long lean form. Caressing, stroking, highlighting the hills and sliding into the valleys. He stroked down her thighs, gently touching the back of her knee.

Instinctively she pulled her leg away. His touch was so sensitive that it was almost ticklish but not.

He reared up suddenly and kissed her lips, catching and holding her as a willing captive.

She wrapped her arms around him and held him close, straddling him on the couch. She didn't know how he had managed it, but she wasn't wearing a stitch, and neither was he. She'd had relationships before, but none where she'd been so mindless—so unaware of what was going on that all she needed was his next kiss, his next touch, his next breath as it mixed with hers.

He tilted her chin to look into her eyes.

Her legs were only half open, her knees clutching his hips, yet she wanted *more*. "More please," she whispered, the corner of her mouth tilting up in a smile.

His gaze deepened, darkened, and he lowered his head to her lips again, turning her so she lay on the couch, his body lowering onto hers.

Her fingers went through his curls, gently stroking, gently caressing, massaging down his back, holding him close, loving the heated skin against skin, the slide, the movement. Everything about this moment seemed so special. Caught in a bubble that hopefully would never burst.

She knew reality was out there, but, for just this moment, the escapism was beyond anything she'd ever experienced. She couldn't get enough of it. She let her hands trail down his back, coming up against his ribs—so much muscle, so much damage. She let her fingers gently slide across the scars, the tips, the pits, the injuries she didn't care about except for what he'd gone through. He lifted his head gasping for air, shuddering in her arms.

She smiled, caressed his cheek and whispered, "You are something." And she kissed him, dropping tiny kisses on the corner of his mouth, gently taking his bottom lip in her mouth and sucking it. He shuddered, and she realized his movements, as practiced and as experienced as they were, were more about a steely self-control. But a self-control that was breaking. There was a wildness in his eyes, and she could see how much he held back. But she didn't want him to hold back. She wanted it all. She wanted every ounce of his passion and his need right here with her.

She tucked him closer, determined to make him lose control, and thrust her tongue deep into his mouth, her hips moving, opening her thighs, wrapping herself around him, and her pelvis pulsating against him in a slow, steady, erotic movement.

He reared back, a cry ripping free of his throat. Without warning, he plunged deep.

She arched her back, a cry of her own escaping, then she froze.

They paused at the top of a hill, both of them testing, waiting, caught up in the experience. His voice was guttural as he asked in a low tone, "Are you okay?"

She laughed, but barely a whisper came out. "I am for the moment. But I won't be if you don't start moving soon."

As if even talking was too much effort, he rose above her on the couch and started to move. Her body welcomed and softened around him with each stroke, letting him in deeper and deeper. Her heart slammed against her chest as she opened her arms to accept him in all ways into her body.

Just as his body tightened and arched, she watched, her eyes open, loving to see that she had brought on this passion, this joy.

And then he surprised her and slid his hand down under her hips, parting her more, as he changed his angle a degree and drove one last time, seating himself right against the heart of her. What started as tiny tremors cascaded into a massive explosion as her own body succumbed to the climax rippling through her. Words were beyond her. She could hear whimpers from somewhere in the room, and, in a dim part of her mind, she realized they came from her. But it was beyond her to control them until the waves stopped crashing on the shores, and she collapsed on the couch, her body never again to be the same.

HE WANTED TO ask her what had just happened, but it would sound too stupid to be believed. His body still thrummed with sexual passion simmering beneath the surface. Then that was kind of the way he'd felt ever since he had first met her. That they lay entwined on the couch was already more than he could have hoped for. But what they had just experienced blew everything he'd ever felt before out of the water. He was collapsed half on top of her, both of them out of space on the small couch, but neither wanting to move.

He heard her murmur, "The bed would be so much more comfortable."

He nuzzled the top of her head and whispered, "Yes, but I will always look at this couch fondly."

Laughter bubbled up from her throat.

He smiled and held her close, but, realizing he would get very heavy, very soon, he gently disengaged himself and stood. She smiled, reached out a hand and gently stroked his hip and his thigh. He held out a hand and said, "Shall we move to the bedroom?"

She sat up and nodded. "Good idea. It's either that or

eat more Chinese food."

"There isn't any more. Once Talon called to say he wasn't coming, we finished it all, remember?" he said with a big smile.

"Darn," she said. "We've worked up an appetite, or at least I have."

"Are you still hungry?" He waggled his eyebrows exaggeratedly.

She chuckled. "Maybe in a few minutes."

He grinned. "I can't wait." Wrapping her shoulders gently in his arms, they walked to the bedroom, the bed covers still disturbed from when she'd gotten up. He pulled them back, waited until she got in and threw them back on top of her. "You do need sleep for tomorrow though," he said, as he got in beside her, tugging her into his arms.

"So do you," she said sleepily. "And I know I need to rest, but, at the same time, I don't want this night to end."

"We could look at it as being the first of many nights," he said, cuddling her close. "Just sleep," he whispered as he watched her eyelids fall closed.

He held her until her breathing evened out and deepened into relaxing sleep. For himself, he felt invigorated. His body alive. It had been more than two years since his accident and even longer since his last relationship. A part of him had wondered if he'd ever get to this point again, if any woman would ever accept the broken pieces of him to get to the man he now was. But Faith didn't seem bothered. He wasn't even sure she would have noticed if he hadn't deliberately pointed out all his flaws. As far as he'd been able to see, she didn't have any—she was perfect.

In the other room, he could hear his phone. He checked the bedside table to see it was two-thirty in the morning. He gently disengaged himself from her arms and slipped out from under the covers again. In the living room, he pulled out his phone to see Talon's message. **Warren Watson has agreed. He's communicating with his contact now.**

He sent him a message back. **Why are you awake?**

Because I'm outside your apartment. Enjoying your night?

Cade smiled. No way would his friends *not* know of the change in his relationship with Faith. But he also knew they'd be happy for him, particularly after Erick and Badger had found two beautiful women, both inside and out, to share their lives with, and Cade was absolutely ecstatic to realize he'd found a third such woman. Somebody who apparently would accept him as he was. He didn't know for how long, he didn't know how deep her feelings ran, but he'd take what he could right now.

He sent back a quick answer. **Absolutely. Thanks.** Then he sat down on the couch for a long moment, wondering if there were any other messages.

As there was nothing else he could do right now, he picked up his phone, grabbed hers and returned to her bedroom. She lay as he had left her. He smiled, placed the phones on the night table beside them, and gently, so as not to disturb her, crawled back under the covers.

Cade could rest with Talon on guard outside. And right now, the only thing that mattered was spending every moment he could with Faith. With that thought in mind, he gently shifted her so she was back in his arms, and he fell asleep.

CHAPTER 14

FAITH OPENED HER eyes, feeling heat she hadn't expected. But, at the sight of Cade's arms wrapped around her, holding her tight, even in sleep protecting her, she realized she'd never felt quite so cosseted or cared for before.

His gravelly voice murmured against her ear, "Are you awake?"

She gave a half nod.

"Finally," he whispered. "I didn't think I'd be able to wait much longer."

And she could feel his erection prodding at her from behind. She gasped as he slid inside and took them on a wild ride that exhausted her but had her gasping for more.

When she recovered, she laughed. "Do you always wake up like that?"

"Only in bed beside you," he admitted. He leaned over and kissed her gently.

She flopped on her back. "I don't know about you, but I need a shower."

He glanced at the clock. "It's seven. We should probably both have a shower. We're about to get company."

She sat up. "Are the guys coming back?"

He shrugged. "I would imagine so. Unless we're meeting somewhere else. But, since you'd be coming with me, it makes sense to have the meeting here."

She bolted off the bed. "In that case I'm running to the shower." She shot him a look that said *alone*. "Otherwise we'll never get out of there," she added on a laugh.

When done, she stepped out of the small room wrapped in a towel, her skin pink and flushed, tendrils of hair still dry but damp from the steam curling around her face.

He leaned forward, kissed her hard and said, "We'll have to have a talk about showering alone."

She patted his cheek. "Another time. There's no way I'm getting caught in the shower with you when those guys are coming." She turned to her closet to find something to wear.

Once dressed, she moved out to the living room and realized Cade had already cleaned up. She put on coffee and checked the fridge to see what there was to feed a hungry man, then mentally corrected that to *hungry men*.

As Cade came out, still towel-drying his hair, she said, "We could meet for breakfast somewhere."

"Right. You haven't been home, so there is no food, is there?"

She shook her head. "No. I did make coffee though."

He handed her her phone while he dialed his. She listened with half an ear as she scrolled through her own messages. He was setting up plans for a breakfast meeting just a couple blocks away. And then she realized there was a message on her phone from Mary.

Thanks for setting the detective on me. Not.

She frowned and realized the detective must have done something. How to respond? She didn't want to engage, but she wanted an update on Elizabeth. She turned to Cade. "Can Laszlo get me an update on Elizabeth?" She held up the message Mary had sent her. "I certainly don't want to answer this."

Cade studied the message and called Laszlo. "I know we're meeting in twenty minutes but any chance we can get an update at the hospital for Elizabeth? Elizabeth's sister, Mary, just sent an odd message to Faith. Something about *Thanks for setting the detective on me.*" He hung up the phone a moment later.

"Does that mean yes or no?" she asked. "I couldn't tell from the conversation."

"He'll call the detective right now."

She smiled with relief. "I'm really glad he speaks Norwegian. Almost everyone has spoken English but there have been a few conversations that went right over my head. Elizabeth taught me a few words, but it's not the easiest of languages."

He grinned. "Not to worry. We should hear back soon."

She walked to the coffeepot and poured two cups. "Well, there is plenty of coffee at the restaurant, but here ..." She handed him a cup. "At least it's fresh right now."

It was also a really small pot. She usually only had two cups in the morning. So this was just enough to kick-start her morning to get them to the restaurant. She collected her purse as she drank her coffee and turned to look at him. "Any chance we can walk?"

He considered the option for a few minutes and then said, "We could."

"But you don't like the idea?" she asked, eyeing him over her coffee cup as she took a sip.

"Out in the open like that, we're slow-moving targets," he said simply.

She frowned and stared down at the thick black brew in her cup. "Well, that puts it in perspective."

"Sorry," he said, his tone low. "I'm not the kind who hides things or makes them all pretty by lying about them."

"Good," she said. "I wouldn't want you to. This is the state we're in. This is what we have to deal with. Let's be smart about it." She looked for her keys, then turned and said, "Where are we going after breakfast?"

"I'm not sure yet. Do you have anything you need to do today?"

"Shop," she said simply. "Particularly if we're staying here for the next couple days. We need food."

He nodded. "Then I'll drive. Although I suspect our hired gunman knows exactly what vehicle you and I both drive."

Frowning, she threw back the rest of her coffee, rinsed out the cup and put it in the sink. He followed suit, and, within seconds, they were outside her apartment door, locking it up, taking the elevator to the ground floor of her complex and now heading toward the parking lot.

She said, "Mine is in my spot. Where are you parked?"

"Out on the road." He led her to his truck, opened the passenger door and closed it behind her. He walked around to his side.

She watched as he got in and started the engine. She buckled in. "Are you not worried about leaving your vehicle out overnight?"

He shrugged. "Talon was on watch last night."

She stared at him wide-eyed. "He watched my place all night?"

Cade nodded. "Yes."

She sat back, a little flummoxed to think somebody had watched over them all night and realized they might or might not have known of their nighttime activities. Nobody could have seen anything through her third-floor windows, but, at the same time, they must have wondered about any sounds that filtered through her open French doors. She didn't know how she felt about that. What she and Cade had going was still too new. It was private. She wasn't sure she wanted anybody to know. And then she realized these men knew each other so well, there was no way they wouldn't know. The only thing she could do was put on a casual and nonchalant face and forget about it.

And, as it was, Talon and Erick never said a word as they walked in. Both had smiles on their faces and warm greetings, but at least they were gentlemen and never brought up how Cade and Faith had spent their night. For that she was grateful.

The waitress brought them cups of coffee and menus. Faith was really hungry and didn't let the waitress leave before ordering her breakfast, already knowing what she wanted. Cade did the same.

The other two men looked up, their gazes going from one to the other, and Erick said in a deadpan voice, "Hungry?"

"Absolutely," she said with a big smile. "I've definitely worked up an appetite." She returned the menu to the waitress and asked for a glass of water at the same time. By the time the woman had disappeared, Faith turned to the men. "So what's happening now?"

"We have a lock on who it is supposedly involved in this, but we must find a way to trap him."

"Hence asking Warren to get involved?" she asked.

Erick nodded. "He has agreed. And I heard this morning from his contact that he is willing too."

"Wow. Okay. That's good then." She smiled. "When

and how?"

"Levi is sending over one of his men. Somebody with a new face and who hasn't been around Santa Fe at all."

"And why one of Levi's men?" she asked.

"Because this hired gunman isn't likely to know him. But Levi's man is a badass and looks like he can handle anything."

"Okay," she said quietly. "And who would that be?"

All the men just looked at each other and then shrugged.

"You don't even know who he is sending?"

"His name is Michael. He's a former SEAL. And a badass in his own right. According to Levi, he can handle this with no problem."

"And is he aware of how dangerous it is?" Faith asked.

Erick nodded. "All of Levi's men do these types of jobs all the time."

She subsided in her chair. "I can't imagine. Once in a lifetime is enough for me."

"This is what these men do."

"How long until he gets here? Or how long until this is set up?"

"Our hit man is in a hurry," Erick said. "I'm hoping it will be soon. It could be this weekend."

"But there's nothing we can do but wait and see?" she asked.

Cade nodded. "But these things can often happen very quickly."

"Not quick enough," she muttered.

The food arrived soon afterward.

Just as she finished eating, she noticed a large man walking in the front door. Something about his face, that look of *take no prisoners*, confirmed he'd been through the wars and had survived.

The man took a seat in the far corner of the restaurant in a booth near a window and ordered coffee. He stared out the window.

She frowned, inching closer to Cade.

He took notice of her movement. "What is it?"

She whispered to Cade, "Now that guy looks dangerous as hell."

His gaze drifted along to see who she was talking about and landed on the man she meant. "Isn't that Geir?" Cade asked the guys, his head nod giving directions.

The men looked toward the last booth, and the stranger turned slowly to stare at them. In a tiny imperceptible movement, he lifted a thumb in acknowledgment and then turned toward the window again.

Faith didn't understand what was going on. But there was excitement on the men's faces. She studied them and spoke in a low voice. "Isn't he one of your men?"

They all nodded.

"So how come you didn't recognize him?"

"The beard," Erick said quietly.

Laszlo nodded. "Exactly."

Just then Talon walked in, also giving their table a discrete thumbs-up. Instead of coming to them, he walked straight over to Geir's booth and sat down. The two men smiled at each other. She could feel the men beside her itching to get over there and to talk with their friend. She motioned to them. "Go. I'm fine here alone."

Cade snorted. "Geir is my buddy. But there's no way in hell I'm leaving you alone."

"Too bad you couldn't use him for this deal. He looks dangerous as hell."

"He is," Erick said in a low tone.

Laszlo laughed. "But still, he's one of us. And is easily recognizable." Laszlo pushed his chair back, got up, walked over and sat down beside Geir, the two of them brushing up in a shoulder bump.

She smiled to see the pleasure on the men's faces. "See? That's what I never had."

"What?" Cade asked, his gaze locked on the men.

She could feel him wanting to go but torn. She sighed. "If the booth over there was bigger, I'd come with you, but there isn't room."

He glanced at her and grinned. He got up, motioned to a waitress. "We'll be joining that man over there."

The men saw them coming, stood, grabbed a small table for two, and pulled it up against the booth. Next thing she knew she was sitting across from one of the most dangerous men she'd ever met in her life. She looked at the hard diamond gaze above the beard and the square-cut jaw hidden underneath the beard, and the power that radiated through-out his frame. She realized this man was on a mission. She didn't know exactly what was going on, but there was rage almost vibrating through his soul. And she realized he had probably just heard about all the accidents and what these guys had been doing, potentially without him.

She placed her hand on his, deliberately covering his metallic-looking prosthesis that rested on the table, and said in a low tone, "I'm Faith. It's nice to meet you, Geir."

He looked at her in surprise for a long moment, his gaze searching. There was almost an uncomfortable intensity to it, and then he glanced down at her fingers and smiled. In a deadly smooth move, he lifted her hand to his lips and kissed her fingers gently. "Welcome to the family."

She smiled. "Thank you."

Geir's gaze wandered to each of them. "What the hell is this, a matchmaking service?" He shook his head. "And here I thought we were on a hunting mission."

Anger hardened his tone, but she understood. She'd seen the shock in Cade's expression when he had found out about his sister. She didn't understand what may have happened in Geir's life, but she knew the accident had already taken a toll. She didn't know if he'd lost a leg or anything else besides his hand, like the other men, but she couldn't imagine how much pain and suffering they'd all been through. She withdrew her hand and laced her fingers with Cade's.

The conversation rolled around her. She listened, only hearing bits and pieces. But they were deliberately not making any reference to anything supersecret.

Just then Erick's phone rang, and the table hushed. She glanced over at Geir to see a muscle twitch in his jaw.

Erick said, "Hello," then listened, a hard look in his eyes.

She sat back, almost willing to distance herself from what was happening. She could see that, whatever it was, it would go down soon.

Erick took a look at his watch and glanced up at Laszlo. "We'll be there." And he hung up. "The meeting is today at four."

"Somebody needs to tell Michael," Cade said.

Geir, in a low voice, asked, "Michael?"

"One of Levi's men," Talon said quietly.

Geir looked at him for a long moment and then nodded. "I know him. Good man." That's all he said.

It seemed like almost immediately everybody turned their thoughts toward the upcoming meeting. But she knew they had a full day to get through. She also realized she was partly the reason why they couldn't talk. They needed to strategize, although they shouldn't do it in a public place. They also didn't quite know what to do with her.

"How about I find some place to visit for the day?" she asked. "Somewhere you'll all be happy that I'm safe and that nobody'll be coming after me, so you guys can set up your plans. Because I can see you're dying to do that." They turned as one and stared at her. She laughed. "Yes, I can see that."

CADE WAS STARTLED at her keen observation skills. "Well, you're right. But we don't have any place to stash you safely."

"How about my place then?" she suggested. "You guys can all sit in the living room, and I'll go to my room, where I can at least read, watch TV or be on my laptop."

The men again exchanged silent glances.

She shrugged. "Or pick some other place. I don't care, but I don't really intend to sit here all day. It's wasting your time. You guys have less than seven hours to set this up properly. Not to mention meet with this other person."

She had no doubt everything would go smoothly today, but that didn't mean there wasn't a need for preparation.

"Four is only a few hours away," Cade said quietly. "You're right. We do need to make some plans." His gaze went from one to the other. "Anybody have a problem with going back to Faith's place?"

As one they shook their heads. Cade stood and held Faith's chair for her. "Then we'll head back now. You guys can come whenever you're ready." He led her back outside. As they stepped out into the fresh air, he said, "Thank you."

She shrugged. "We had to do something. It's obvious you guys need to talk, and I'm in the way."

"It's not that you're in the way, but it's not the kind of talk we normally have with other people around."

"So, it's not a trust issue?"

Startled, he stared at her. "No. It's not that we don't trust you. But it's much better if you don't know anything at all."

"Whatever. Let's just go home. I can do laundry and change the bed. I'm sure there's any number of things I can keep myself busy with at home. But I'm not cooking for everybody," she warned.

At that, he chuckled. "That's not a problem."

They were soon back at her apartment. He made sure the place was clear as they walked in the building and up to her apartment. As they stepped inside, he went in first and did a quick search, but it was as they had left it.

She went to her bedroom and called back, "Let me know when I can come out." She closed the door gently in front of him.

He winced. This had to be difficult for her. He needed to give her as much space as possible, but, at the same time, it was a little tough. He wanted to crawl back into bed with her and make all this go away.

But it wouldn't go away. As a matter of fact, he was caught up in something that was years in the making. If they could get any answers, he needed to get them now.

The doorbell rang. He walked over and opened it, letting Erick and Talon in. Within ten minutes the entire group was seated. "Anybody heard from Michael?"

Erick nodded. "He's in Santa Fe. He preferred to have the meeting earlier, but it is what it is." He shrugged. "Given the location, which is also another hotel, we need to plan how we'll back Michael up."

"Did he come alone?"

Erick shook his head. "Several of the men from his old unit are with him."

Geir nodded. "I know them too. Sounds like Levi has hired himself some really good men."

"He has," Laszlo said quietly. "I'd consider it myself, if I was a little more whole."

Geir had a serious look at his face. "You'll be just fine the way you are. He's got Stone, and Stone doesn't mind anyone knowing about his missing leg."

"I know, but I'm not sure I'm up for the same level of expertise and action that we were in before."

"I hear you there, but I want five minutes with this asshole," Geir said. "I want to know if this was what was going on for these last couple years and if he had anything to do with our original accident. For a long time, I wondered. I started doing my own investigation, thinking surely this reality had to have been contrived. That somehow we hadn't screwed up so bad. That the world didn't hate us so much. But to think somebody got away with it just eats me up. And then when I heard from Erick about these *accidents*..." He couldn't finish speaking. His jaw locked, and he ran out of words, his gaze obsidian hard.

Cade understood. There was no easy answer here. "We'll get answers," he said. "You can count on it."

Geir gave one short quick nod. "I *am* counting on it. That's why I'm here."

Cade glanced back at Erick. "Still no word on Jager?"

Erick shook his head. "Not yet."

"I'd feel better if he'd at least check in. He had nothing to do with it, I know. But it'd be nice if we were all at least together and not one off alone on a vigilante mission."

"I don't think he's doing that at all," Talon said. "Jager was always the best of us at night hunting. And, if he's gone dark, you can bet he's gone dark all the way. As long as somebody is feeding him intel, we need to know what he's up to. So we're not reproducing the same work because we don't have the time or the energy or the funds for that," he said. "Jager will keep doing his thing. And eventually we'll track this guy down who has done this to our unit, to our families."

Erick's phone buzzed. He read the message, "Michael is at the hotel."

"Already?"

"He got a second message, saying the meeting was to move ahead to noon." Everybody checked their watches. "It's ten now. That's only two hours."

Immediately they brought up the blueprints of the hotel and set about coming up with a plan.

"I doubt the hired gunman will be taken alive," Laszlo said. "We have to consider that."

The men nodded.

"I want him alive long enough to answer questions."

"I doubt he will be for long. Either way, we must make sure he's stopped."

"Gotcha. It would be nice to have some personal belongings to go through, a computer, laptop, cell phone too."

Erick's phone rang again. "Michael again," he exclaimed. "He just got another message. Our target wants the meeting as soon as possible now that he knows Michael is in town."

"He can't go in alone," Laszlo said urgently. "Don't let him do that."

Erick jumped to his feet. "We're about twenty minutes away from that hotel. I suggest we get moving." He turned to look at Cade. "You need to stay here with Faith."

Cade's fist closed.

"If the guy is at the airport hotel, then *she* doesn't need protection here." The words came from behind them.

Cade turned to see Faith in the doorway, her arms crossed. "Take him. Just make sure nobody here gets hurt again. I'm fine. I'll have the door locked. And, yes, I'll text if anything should even bark outside."

Cade didn't know what to do. She was right, in the sense that, if this guy was at the hotel, she should be safe, but he didn't want to take that chance either. As he looked at the men, he realized just how many of them there were to go after one guy. "You're right. I'll stay here."

Faith rushed to his side. "No. This is too important. You need answers before you can move on. I'm not part of your past. I'm part of your future. But, in order to have it, you must deal with your past. Now go." And she wouldn't listen to any other arguments.

Within minutes they were out of the apartment. They took three different vehicles, approaching the hotel from three different sides.

Inside, Cade's stomach was in knots. He said to Erick, "I still hate to leave her alone."

"As long as she stays locked up, she should be fine. We'll be back in no time."

Cade nodded, but it still felt wrong. He hated to see anything happen to her. They pulled into the hotel parking lot. As he went to get out, Erick pulled him back in.

"Remember, this guy knows who we are. We can't have him see us and throw this off. Michael is already very skilled at this. He can take down this asshole. It's just that we want to make sure we're there right afterward. We're the insurance that nothing happens to Michael and his team. But it's Michael and his team who are taking down the hired gun."

Cade took a deep breath and settled back. "Thanks, I needed that reminder. I wanted to go in there and rip this asshole limb from limb."

"I know. But that doesn't mean it'll happen."

The two men sat in the vehicle. Cade could feel his nerves clenching his gut and constricting his chest. He wanted to bolt inside. But Michael was meeting in the restaurant. Just a business meeting between two men. His buddies would already be inside, having searched out the restaurant first. And Cade wanted to go in and have a seat at the table himself. But, if this guy knew them, Cade would completely mess up the project.

Cade checked his watch. Five minutes to the meeting time. He rubbed his temple. "Of all the missions in the world we have completed, this one has my guts in a knot."

"Because something will go wrong?"

Cade shook his head. "Because I want this guy so goddamn bad."

"Ditto."

Laszlo had done a walk-through in the hotel lobby. He was an expert at disguises. They were waiting for his call to tell them if the meeting was on.

The time clicked by on the clock. The dashboard digital light flickered ever so goddamn slowly that Cade wanted to pound it to make sure it was still working.

Finally they got a message from Laszlo on Erick's phone.

It's on.

They sat back, and a breath of relief gusted out of Erick's chest. "Thank God," he whispered. "I was afraid the guy wouldn't show at the last minute."

"We'll take him down," Cade said. "We need a place that's private to hold him."

"That won't happen. I wouldn't mind taking him out in the restaurant," Erick said. "There are boardrooms. As they separate, I suggest we maneuver him into one of those. It's not like he'll be able to fight back."

"No, it'll have to be outside," Cade stated. "Otherwise we'll end up involved in hotel security, and then we'll have the cops all over us."

"Good point," Erick said. "Let's bag and tag him, and toss him in the truck and move."

"As long as we're not seen," Cade said. "What we need to do is make sure this is handled as quietly as possible."

A second text came in. **Meeting is over.**

They exited the vehicle and walked up to the front of the hotel. Michael was a pro. While they could trust that Michael knew how to handle any situation, they couldn't take for granted the fact that this hired gun was a wild card, one who appeared to be doing very well for himself.

He walked out and headed straight for the elevator. Interesting. The men slipped into the stairwell as Michael appeared to walk out the front door. He never looked back.

Outside he got out his phone.

Inside the stairwell they could still see Michael. Erick answered the call. "What happened?"

"Deal is done. I have the money. Now pick him up."

"Any idea where he's staying?"

"Sixth floor."

Erick was already running. "And your men?"

"They're on the sixth floor." Michael's voice was dry when he said, "Don't shoot them."

"Where are you going?"

"I'm carrying ten million dollars. I'm not going very far."

Cade raced up the stairs. "Ten million, Jesus."

"I know, right?" Erick said to Cade, while still holding the phone so Michael could hear their end.

"But this guy is not likely to stay at the hotel for long," Cade said, his breathing a little winded as they neared the sixth floor.

"Just long enough to complete his business," Erick added. "And then where the hell is he going?"

"I didn't ask him," Michael said.

At the sixth floor they opened the door to see a stranger walking down from the far end. It wasn't the man they were looking for. Just then a hotel room door opened. They headed toward it. And sure enough, it was their bearded hired gunman coming out with a laptop and briefcase in his hands. He looked up, saw them, dropped what he held to reach into his jacket, as Cade and Erick rushed him, pushing him back into the room.

He glared at them and freed his gun from his shoulder holster.

Cade and Erick both saw the move coming. Cade grabbed the gun-toting arm and squeezed, the man releasing his grip and the gun dropping in Cade's other hand, while Erick kicked him in the knee.

The hired gunman dropped to all fours on the floor, glaring at them.

The two men snorted as Laszlo and Talon slipped in

from the back.

The hired gun sneered at them all. "Nothing but a bunch of wounded ex-warriors."

Cade reached over and casually smacked him across the face. And he used his prosthetic hand to do it. The man stared at Cade's arm, his hand going instinctively to his cheek. And that's when Cade saw the scars and scratches on the back of his hand. Just as Faith had said. And there … he studied the look in the man's eyes and saw the same thing the gas station attendant had seen—a cold and dead look. And dead was what Cade would be if this guy ever got the upper hand. His gaze promised retribution for this atrocity.

"Where did you get the ten million?" Erick asked.

The man's eyebrows rose, while a smirk curled his lips. "What ten million?"

Erick laughed. "It doesn't matter. Because the money is ours now."

The man's haughty glare never diminished. "Money won't help you guys."

The men shrugged. Cade grabbed the hired gunman, pinned his arms behind his back as the others searched him. He had a small handgun in his left sock but nothing more under his jacket. They pulled out his wallet and checked his name, confirmed it was the same as they had seen many times already. And his wallet was stuffed full of cash. Erick pulled it out, shuffled it through his fingers and whistled. "There are thousands in here alone."

"Petty cash. Take it," the hired gun said. "Buy yourselves a new life."

The men just glared at him and remained silent.

But Laszlo already had the hired gun's briefcase and the laptop. "He says that's petty cash. Take a look at this." He flipped the briefcase around, and, sure enough, it was stacked full of cash.

The men stared at the cash and then at the hired gunman, and Cade said, "We need to have a talk."

The man chuckled, then shrugged.

Laszlo opened the laptop and booted it up. "It won't matter if he talks or not. This laptop should tell us what we want to know."

"Look. It was a job," the hired gun said. "That's all it was. It was a job."

Hearing their loved ones cut down for "work" in exchange for money was beyond a slap in the face.

Several of the men took a deep breath and stepped back, realizing how close to the edge they'd all come. Laszlo had the laptop up and booted. "He's got it locked with a password."

"I know what it is," Cade said instinctively.

Laszlo turned toward him and frowned. "What?"

"Try the word, *Mouse*." Cade had uttered the words, but the hired gunman still had a lot of explaining to do.

CHAPTER 15

S HE HATED WAITING, but Faith didn't have much more in the way of options. She wanted to text Cade to see how things had gone down, but she knew it could be the worst thing she could do right now.

This really had nothing to do with her. She just hoped that, at the end of it all, he'd come back, and she'd be safe.

As she sat on the couch, her phone rang. She checked the Caller ID to see it was Mary. She frowned. "Hello, Mary. What's up? Is Elizabeth okay?"

Instead Elizabeth's shaky voice said, "Hey, girlfriend."

Faith burst into tears. "Oh, my God! You're awake!" she cried out, laughing and cheering. She jumped to her feet, dashing around the living room.

"I am. I'm still pretty weak, but I'm awake. And I survived, which I'll put down in part to your presence."

Faith started to bawl. "Oh, my God! It's been so tough not knowing what was happening with you."

"I'm fine. Or I will be," Elizabeth amended cheekily. "I woke up a couple hours ago. I didn't even know what had happened. The doctors have been talking to me, and the nurses have all told me about you sitting here for days until Mary insisted you be kicked out." Elizabeth's voice cracked. "I'm so sorry."

"I was horrified. I felt so betrayed and so helpless," Faith said, rubbing her face, wiping away the tears coursing down her cheeks. "I didn't know how to defend you when I was not even allowed to be there."

"And I heard you. In a weird way, I heard you calling to me. You were talking about our childhood, the things we got into trouble for and the things we did together."

"Yes," Faith cried out. "That's exactly what I was doing." She sat down for a moment in awe, quietly sobbing. "I'm so happy you heard me."

"Me too," Elizabeth said with a laugh. "I don't know what your schedule is like right now. And I'm definitely not in any way ready to have company, but maybe, when I do get back on my feet, we could take some time off together."

With Faith still sobbing quietly, they made plans to talk a little more, and then Elizabeth said, "I have to get off the phone now. I'm not allowed to do too much. But I wouldn't go to sleep tonight until I'd had a chance to connect with you." And with that Elizabeth rang off.

Faith sat for a long moment, clutching the phone to her chest, so overwhelmed with joy that she couldn't fathom it all. She had so many questions to ask. She presumed the sisters were at least talking, and that's how Elizabeth had managed to call from Mary's phone.

At the same time, Faith wasn't sure she'd ever be able to forgive Mary for what she had put Elizabeth—and Faith—through. It just wasn't fair. She sobbed quietly, letting the relief and pain for the last few weeks wash over her.

Curled up on the couch, she finally fell into a light doze. She woke up when there was an odd sound outside and realized it was the men coming back.

She glanced at her phone as she walked toward the front door, hearing the doorbell ring. There was a message from

Cade saying it was all over. The men were returning and bringing food.

She laughed. This was the best day ever. She could hear them outside and realized she must have fallen asleep longer than she supposed at first. It was two o'clock. She opened the door to see a complete stranger standing there. She smiled up at him. "Hi."

He smiled at her. "Hi. I have a message for Cade. Can you give it to him for me?"

She nodded and beamed. "Of course I can. What is it?"

He said, "It's a simple phrase. If you could remember to tell him, *How is Mouse?* That's all." And then he waved at her, turned and walked down the hall.

Sleepy, it took her a minute to remember how important that name was. She frowned after him, realizing Cade would absolutely shoot her for opening the door. But the man disappeared down the stairwell. She hadn't recognized him at all.

Just then her phone rang. She turned, closed and locked the front door, then answered the phone to find Cade calling. "Are you okay?" came his voice.

"Elizabeth phoned me."

"Elizabeth?" he said. "From Norway? She's awake?"

Laughing and crying at the same time, she told him about Elizabeth's call.

"Did she say anything about why Mary did what she did?"

"No, she just told me that she could hear me and what I'd been saying. She said she wasn't allowed to talk on the phone for very long."

"Excellent," he said. "I'm so happy for you."

"I know. Me too." She looked at the clock. "Are you

guys done yet?"

"We're going through the guy's laptop now. We have the money. We have everything, but he's not talking."

"Of course not. He's killed a lot of people."

"The trouble is, we don't know exactly who he's killed. But it is the same guy who was in Norway."

"Right. Now don't be mad. I saw the text message that you were picking up food and that you would come here."

"Sure, but not for a little while yet."

"Oh, I didn't see that part of the message," she said. "But I heard noises outside, so I opened the door. There was a man standing there. I was expecting you. He said he had a message for you."

"What? You opened the door without checking?"

She winced. "Remember that part about don't get mad?" At his ominous tone on the other end of the phone, she said, "Look. It's okay. He's gone. But he had a message for you."

"For me?"

"Yes. His message was, *How is Mouse?* That's all he said, and then he turned and walked away with a hand wave."

There was dead silence on the other side of the phone.

"Cade?" she asked nervously. "Are you okay?"

"No," he said, his voice glacial. "We'll talk about it later. But if you open that door to anybody else but me, then you will have to face me when I get there." His tone was beyond angry. "Do you understand? Likely you were just talking to the man who hired our hit man."

CADE TURNED TO face the men and to stare at the hit man still on the floor, still not saying a word. He didn't appear to be biding his time, waiting to make an escape, though they couldn't trust him. Cade said, "Somebody just went to Faith's door and left a message for me."

Instantly the men frowned.

"She opened the door to a stranger?"

He shot Laszlo a hard look. "Yes. And you know that we'll have something to say about that when we get there. But for the moment, the message he left was *How is Mouse?*"

The men all stiffened.

"Son of a bitch," Laszlo said. He turned the laptop around. "I'm in."

There in front of Cade was a photo of his sister. She sat in the vehicle, blood on her forehead, the door open, nobody else around. He turned to look at the hired gunman and slammed his fist into the man's face.

Without a word, the hired gun toppled over sideways, unconscious.

Cade stared at the picture of his sister again, his heart breaking. "He really did kill her." Cade forced himself to walk to the door. He was so frustrated and angry and so full of grief that he wanted to smash open the hired gun's head against something hard. But he knew it wouldn't be just his grief. If this asshole had done what they suspected he'd done, that meant he was also involved in so much more.

Erick patted Cade's shoulder. "Remember, it's not just you."

"There are also confirmations of his flights to Norway." Laszlo twisted the laptop around to show pictures of his father on the side of the road just seconds after the car had hit him.

"Laszlo, keep going through his laptop to see how many other hits he's been involved in," Cade said, "but it's obvious the money came from doing these jobs."

"Do we hand him over to the police?" Talon asked.

Laszlo shook his head. "I wouldn't. But I think we should take him out of here to one of our places and hold him until we've asked him whatever questions we need to ask."

"And we need to put a rush on it," Erick said. "Because, if the boss man who hired this guy was just at Faith's apartment, he also knows this guy is here. He'll do everything he can to stop us from talking to him."

At the knock on the door, the men instantly went quiet. Cade checked the peephole, opened the door. Michael walked in and introduced the two men beside him as Brandon and Liam. "Well, you got him. Has he got any information for you?"

Talon said, "He's not talking."

"Not while he's unconscious, he's not," Michael quipped.

"Where's Geir, by the way?" Cade looked around. "I thought he'd be here."

"He's staying outside, said he didn't trust himself not to beat the shit out of him for what happened to everyone."

"I won't find the answers I need right away," Laszlo said. "The laptop is full of information. I can only back up so much, and I don't really want to do it here. We don't know what else this guy's got planned."

"And for how long."

"Then we move him. We pick one of our places, and we move him."

The men quickly discussed options for the next two minutes before coming to a solution. Although it wasn't the best idea, it was a workable one. There was a motel between

Faith's place and Badger's. It was on the city side of town, but, for this purpose, it would work. All they had to do was get the hired gunman over there and get him conscious. The chances were, they could keep the prisoner for a couple days while they figured this out. And somebody would have to talk to the cops, bring them in on it, but they wanted to make sure they got the information they needed off the laptop first.

As the hired gun woke up and saw Michael in front of him, his features twisted in anger. "I knew you were too good to be true," he snarled.

The atmosphere of the hotel room was intense. There was just so much anger, so much rage surging through the room. Cade knew it was dangerous. He stepped back and pointed at the hired gun. "You need to start talking, and you need to start talking now."

He snorted, gave a one-shoulder shrug. "I can't talk."

Cade knew exactly what he would say next. "Why not?"

"He'll kill me."

"Well, if he doesn't, we will," Erick said smoothly. "I doubt there's anything you can say to us that'll stop our anger."

Cade knew there were tears that needed to be shed. But, at the same time, he couldn't break down now. He looked around the room.

Michael stepped before the hired gun. "You're the asshole who took out my friends' family members and the one who arranged for a land mine to blow up their truck, injuring all these men and killing Mouse."

The man's face froze, and he stared at them. "Whoa! I didn't have anything to do with that."

Michael raised an eyebrow, crossed his arms over his

chest. "Prove it." He nodded to each of the men. "Every one of them went through two years of hell because of you."

Cade interjected, "And you killed one of our unit."

The man held up his hands. "I had nothing to do with that. Nothing to do with a military operation. That was the other guy."

Everyone froze.

"The other guy?" Laszlo asked, his voice soft, deadly.

"The guy who hired me. He gave me three specific jobs. I figured the targets had to be related somehow. After I asked him about it, he told me to shut the hell up and that he was working on a bigger plan."

"And if you didn't shut up?"

The hit man's face twisted. "Why the hell do you think I was getting the money out of the country? I needed to leave. This last job and the boss ..." He shook his head. "When he told me, I knew it was over. I would be next on his list. And then you guys nabbed me. If he finds out—"

Crack.

The glass balcony door shattered. The men scattered. Cade hit the floor. There was almost no room. There were bodies on top of bodies. But it had been a single shot. And he knew. As he stood, he knew. He looked over at the hired gunman.

The bullet had gone right through his head.

"God damn it," Cade said, pulling on his hair. "At least now we know."

"Now we know what?" Talon cried. "We know there's still one more asshole. When does this end?"

"There's at least one more. If we can't prove this hired gun orchestrated all seven accidents, there's somebody else. And it could be the boss, or it could be another hired gun."

"Well, we know for sure we'll have the cops involved now. So we need everything off that laptop that we can get."

"And the money?"

The men stared at the money with distaste.

"I have no idea," Erick said. "We'll put in a claim with the cops. Maybe we can give it to a charity. It was blood money. And we all paid the price."

The men scrambled.

Cade turned to Michael and his two cohorts. "I suggest you leave this mess to us."

Michael nodded. "But tell the cops who I am. And they're welcome to contact me about my role."

With that Michael and his friends left.

Cade turned to look at the others. "Somebody will have to handle this."

Erick exhaled a long-drawn-out sigh. "I will. We already have a detective involved in the Norway matter. I'll bring him in on this one too." He looked at Laszlo. "Laszlo, take the laptop. Leave the money, and let's go through the briefcase before you leave, so we take photos of any information we need. I'll stay here and handle this." He turned to Cade. "Cade, go home. Obviously, Faith needs a stronger warning next time. And you also might want to consider the fact that now she can't be left alone *ever*. He not only knows who she is, he knows where she is. And she can identify him."

Cade gave him a quick nod. "I'll be moving her into my place today."

"Good luck with that." He took one last look at the dead hired gunman. "Laszlo, I want to see that laptop too. Later."

"I'm coming with you now," Laszlo told Cade. And they left.

As they walked outside, Laszlo said, "I have my wheels. Want me to drop you off at Faith's?"

Cade nodded. "Yes, I left my truck at her place."

"Don't be too hard on her."

Cade sighed. "No, I won't. She doesn't live in the world we live in. And she was so excited because Elizabeth woke up and called her."

Laszlo looked at him in surprise. "That's excellent news. Does that mean you're heading back to Norway?"

Cade laughed. "I have no idea. My head's still spinning in high speed with everything happening now. I don't know where she and I are at."

Laszlo smiled as they got into the vehicle and headed toward Faith's apartment. "Don't rush it. You have time. This beginning stage is special. Make it last."

CHAPTER 16

W HEN THE DOORBELL rang, she checked out the peephole and saw Cade, a very tired Cade, standing on the other side. She opened the door, and he opened his arms. She stepped in wordlessly. He just held her.

After a moment he gently pushed her inside and closed the door.

She asked, "Is it over?"

He winced and whispered, "Some of it is over. I'll explain later. But, for the moment, I just want to hold you."

She wrapped her arms around him. "I'm so sorry."

"What for?"

"For opening the door to that man, for your sister, for all of it." And she just held him.

He smiled, kissed the top of her head and said, "You know what I'm not sorry about?"

She tilted her head to look up at him, and he smiled down at her.

"For you. I'm so grateful you've come into my life."

She smiled mistily. "I don't know what happened to you, with that mess today, but I have to admit, with Elizabeth waking up and you saying that, it's been one of the best days of my life."

He leaned forward and kissed her again. "The first of many to come."

She smiled and snuggled in close, and he realized that they had made a huge stride forward. Even though the bearded hired gunman was dead, Cade would never have wanted this murdering asshole to go to trial. He wouldn't have wanted his sister's case to be all over the media. In many ways this was the best answer ever. But he was so damn frustrated to know they still had been kept from the boss man at the top.

But Laszlo was a genius with computers, and they had a lot of information to handle right now. And they could find out so much more. Like Faith said, it was a good day. And he'd stand by that anytime.

As he cuddled the woman in his arms, he realized it was better than a good day. It really was one of the best days. He tilted her head back and kissed her, so damn grateful to have her in his arms again.

EPILOGUE

T WENTY MINUTES AFTER leaving the craziness at the hotel, Talon Lore knocked at the front door but didn't wait to walk into Laszlo's small Santa Fe rented house.

Laszlo was already there, working on the dead hired gun's laptop. Laszlo waved to Talon and said, "Put on your own coffee."

Talon snorted. "We walked out and left Erick to deal with the cops."

"That's all right," Geir said as he walked inside from the back door without so much as knocking. "If there was ever anybody who could handle it, it'd be Erick."

Talon studied his friend. "How are you holding up?"

Geir extended both hands, still shaking with fury. "I didn't dare go in that room."

Talon nodded. "I understand. It's all okay though. We're working our way through this. One new fact at a time."

"And faster than I would have thought," Laszlo said. "It's just these hiccups are pretty damn ugly."

"I'm also pissed you guys didn't tell me right away what you were doing," Geir said. "I had to hear after the fact."

"Hey," Talon said, "you went silent. We've been trying to reach you."

"Besides," Laszlo added, "we all heard after the fact, in a

way. Badger wouldn't ever let it go. It's been bugging him for the last two years. He caught the first lead, and we carried on down the rabbit hole from there."

Geir nodded. "Just so long as I'm in the loop from here on in."

"You're in," Talon said. "But remember, you may not want to be."

"Like you guys," Geir said, "my life hasn't moved forward. It always felt so wrong, and I couldn't find a way to get back on track."

"Well, we might have something to help you get there." Laszlo lifted his gaze from the laptop. "Because there's a lot of stuff here. It looks like we have more than enough information to confirm this John Smith asshole was a very busy boy. Not just with our cases but others. The police will still want to see this laptop. But I want to get all the information I need off it first."

"Does it say who he did business with?"

"A couple people could be in here. It's in code, and it'll take us some time. Do we have any specialists we can bring in?"

Geir snorted. "If Levi doesn't have them, you know Mason will."

Talon nodded. "And what about my friend Chad? Is there any sign this hired gun had anything to do with Chad's accident?"

Laszlo nodded. "Yes." He looked up. "I don't know how well you know the family. Do you want to say anything to them about it or let it lie in peace after all this time?"

Talon winced. "His sister and I were a thing for a long time, and Chad was my best friend. I feel like I owe her the truth for the sake of both of them."

"Clary?" Geir asked. "I remember you mentioning her a couple times. Why did you break it off?"

Talon shrugged. "Because I couldn't leave the military at the time. And she wanted me home every night," he admitted. "And I let her go because she wanted so much more than I could give her."

"How do you feel about her now?" Laszlo looked up from the laptop again, his gaze piercing, even in the darkly lit room.

"I've never forgotten her," Talon said. "But she married soon after we broke up. I figured she was more than ready for the change."

"Well, maybe it's time to renew that acquaintance."

He shook his head. "No, she's happily married. I don't want to burst that bubble."

Laszlo snorted, his fingers busy on the keyboard. "No, she's not. She got divorced last year."

Talon straightened ever-so-slightly. "Really?"

Laszlo nodded. "Really. And I think she deserves to know the truth. At least what we know of the truth. Chad was walking in a parking lot and was struck by a hit-and-run driver."

"Another vehicular accident," Geir said softly. "Son of a bitch."

Laszlo snorted. "Talon, looks like you're up next."

Talon nodded. "Maybe I am at that."

This concludes Book 3 of SEALs of Steel: Cade.
Read about Talon: SEALs of Steel, Book 4

SEALS OF STEEL: TALON BOOK 4

When an eight-man unit hit a landmine, all were injured but one died. The remaining seven aim to see his death avenged.

Talon's best friend's murder ties in with the landmine incident. Talon walked away from Clary a year ago. She was his best friend's sister, and he vows to keep her safe.

Clary regrets losing Talon, but love—not trouble—needs to be his reason for staying...even if sending him away jeopardizes her life.

Book 4 is available now!

To find out more visit Dale Mayer's website.

http://smarturl.it/dmtalon

Author's Note

Thank you for reading Cade: SEALs of Steel, Book 3! If you enjoyed the book, please take a moment and leave a short review.

Dear reader,

I love to hear from readers, and you can contact me at my website: www.dalemayer.com or at my Facebook author page. To be informed of new releases and special offers, sign up for my newsletter or follow me on BookBub. And if you are interested in joining Dale Mayer's Fan Club, here is the Facebook sign up page.
facebook.com/groups/402384989872660

Cheers,
Dale Mayer

Your Free Book Awaits!

KILL OR BE KILLED

Part of an elite SEAL team, Mason takes on the dangerous jobs no one else wants to do – or can do. When he's on a mission, he's focused and dedicated. When he's not, he plays as hard as he fights.

Until he meets a woman he can't have but can't forget. Software developer, Tesla lost her brother in combat and has no intention of getting close to someone else in the military. Determined to save other US soldiers from a similar fate, she's created a program that could save lives. But other countries know about the program, and they won't stop until they get it – and get her.

Time is running out ... For her ... For him ... For them ...

DOWNLOAD a ***complimentary*** copy of MASON? Just tell me where to send it!

http://dalemayer.com/sealsmason/

About the Author

Dale Mayer is a USA Today bestselling author best known for her Psychic Visions and Family Blood Ties series. Her contemporary romances are raw and full of passion and emotion (Second Chances, SKIN), her thrillers will keep you guessing (By Death series), and her romantic comedies will keep you giggling (It's a Dog's Life and Charmin Marvin Romantic Comedy series).

She honors the stories that come to her – and some of them are crazy and break all the rules and cross multiple genres!

To go with her fiction, she also writes nonfiction in many different fields with books available on resume writing, companion gardening and the US mortgage system. She has recently published her Career Essentials Series. All her books are available in print and ebook format.

Connect with Dale Mayer Online

Dale's Website – www.dalemayer.com

Twitter – @DaleMayer

Facebook – facebook.com/DaleMayer.author

BookBub – bookbub.com/authors/dale-mayer

Also by Dale Mayer

Published Adult Books:

Psychic Vision Series
Tuesday's Child
Hide 'n Go Seek
Maddy's Floor
Garden of Sorrow
Knock Knock...
Rare Find
Eyes to the Soul
Now You See Her
Shattered
Into the Abyss
Seeds of Malice
Eye of the Falcon
Itsy-Bitsy Spider
Psychic Visions Books 1–3
Psychic Visions Books 4–6
Psychic Visions Books 7–9

By Death Series
Touched by Death
Haunted by Death
Chilled by Death
By Death Books 1–3

Charmin Marvin Romantic Comedy Series
Broken Protocols
Broken Protocols 2
Broken Protocols 3
Broken Protocols 3.5
Broken Protocols 1-3

Broken and... Mending
Skin
Scars
Scales (of Justice)
Broken but... Mending 1-3

Glory
Genesis
Tori
Celeste
Glory Trilogy

Biker Blues
Biker Blues: Morgan, Part 1
Biker Blues: Morgan, Part 2
Biker Blues: Morgan, Part 3
Biker Baby Blues: Morgan, Part 4
Biker Blues: Morgan, Full Set
Biker Blues: Salvation, Part 1
Biker Blues: Salvation, Part 2
Biker Blues: Salvation, Part 3
Biker Blues: Salvation, Full Set

SEALs of Honor
Mason: SEALs of Honor, Book 1

Heroes for Hire

Jace's Jewel: Heroes for Hire, Book 11
Rory's Rose: Heroes for Hire, Book 12
Brandon's Bliss: Heroes for Hire, Book 13
Liam's Lily: Heroes for Hire, Book 14
Heroes for Hire, Books 1–3
Heroes for Hire, Books 4–6
Heroes for Hire, Books 7–9

SEALs of Steel
Badger: SEALs of Steel, Book 1
Erick: SEALs of Steel, Book 2
Cade: SEALs of Steel, Book 3
Talon: SEALs of Steel, Book 4

Collections
Dare to Be You…
Dare to Love…
Dare to be Strong…
RomanceX3

Standalone Novellas
It's a Dog's Life
Riana's Revenge
Second Chances

Published Young Adult Books:

Family Blood Ties Series
Vampire in Denial
Vampire in Distress
Vampire in Design
Vampire in Deceit

Vampire in Defiance
Vampire in Conflict
Vampire in Chaos
Vampire in Crisis
Vampire in Control
Vampire in Charge
Family Blood Ties Set 1–3
Family Blood Ties Set 1–5
Family Blood Ties Set 4–6
Family Blood Ties Set 7–9
Sian's Solution, A Family Blood Ties Series Prequel
    Novelette

Design series
Dangerous Designs
Deadly Designs
Darkest Designs
Design Series Trilogy

Standalone
In Cassie's Corner
Gem Stone (a Gemma Stone Mystery)
Time Thieves

Published Non-Fiction Books:

Career Essentials
Career Essentials: The Résumé
Career Essentials: The Cover Letter
Career Essentials: The Interview
Career Essentials: 3 in 1

CPSIA information can be obtained
at www.ICGtesting.com
Printed in the USA
FFHW011034050819
54104206-59797FF

9 781773 360782